SCENT OF DEATH

A CHRISTIAN ROMANTIC SUSPENSE

SULLIVAN K9 SEARCH AND RESCUE

LAURA SCOTT

1

Alexis Sullivan kept pace with her K9, a black and white border collie, Denali as they moved through the Bighorn Mountains. This search area was new for them, a slight deviation from where her older sister Jessica and her now husband, Logan, had found the piece of tail fin they believed came from their parents' plane crash.

"Search napoo!" she called encouragingly. Not that Denali showed signs of slowing down. Her K9 loved to work, despite their mission being to find human remains. The term *napoo* meant finished, done, dead. And all cadaver handlers used the term rather than telling their dog to search for dead bodies.

Despite the grim task, Alexis had purposefully

chosen this area of expertise to help during natural disasters. She and Denali had worked from wildfire sites in California to tornado wrecks in North Carolina. The fact that her parents had never been found after their small plane had crashed over five years ago now had also factored into her decision. Which was why she was here in the mountains working with her K9.

Denali swept her keen nose over the ground as they walked. Alexis worked alone today, as summer was the busiest time for the Sullivan K9 Search and Rescue Ranch. Everyone else was out and about doing things. She was the middle child of nine siblings, all of whom worked with dogs in various specialties. Denali was the only cadaver dog on the ranch, though, so this specific task wasn't something the other K9s could help with.

The sound of a dead tree branch snapping had her whirling around to scan the foliage behind her. Probably a large elk or a bear moving through the woods. She lightly touched the can of bear spray on her utility belt to reassure herself she was ready if needed.

She carried a firearm, too, and her oldest brother, Chase, had made sure every one of the Sullivan siblings could shoot accurately. But a small handgun may not be enough to take down a bear, unless she was able to hit the animal in the heart or brain.

Not that she wanted to kill a bear or any other wild animal for that matter. She understood and accepted the hunting her brothers did, and she didn't even mind eating venison and elk meat, but the actual hunting part wasn't something she personally enjoyed.

Seeing nothing alarming, she rolled her shoulders beneath the heavy pack and tried to relax. Turning, she continued up the mountain. Denali was still working through the brush, her nose sniffing along the ground. Her dog was so good she'd picked up the scent of human ashes while working in California. Many cadaver K9s couldn't do that. Even so, sometimes Alexis wondered if searching for her parents' remains was a fruitless effort. What could possibly be left of them after five and a half years?

Yet she couldn't just give up either. After Jessica had found the tail fin of a plane, she and her siblings had renewed their search efforts. Especially since the piece of plane debris had been found a good fifty miles from their original search zone.

Why her parents' small plane had gone down was a mystery. Their youngest sibling, Kendra, kept insisting the crash was no accident. And while

Alexis may secretly agree, the problem was that there was no motive to kill her parents.

Well, there was the fact that her parents had been worth millions of dollars, something she and the other siblings hadn't known until after they'd been declared dead. The money was in a trust that covered the expenses of the ranch in addition to a modest salary for each of the siblings. Maya and Chase, the two eldest siblings, held family meetings every six months to go over the finances. Somehow, the trust continued to grow despite the difficult economic times. The money would have been a motive to kill her parents if not for the fact that her parents had everything buttoned up in the trust, and the only heirs were the nine kids.

As far as she knew, nobody had tried to get the money from them. In fact, the Sullivan family had managed to keep the extent of their wealth a secret. Turning the former dude ranch into a search and rescue operation had been Maya's idea. Chase had eagerly agreed. They performed SAR services across the state of Wyoming, even venturing into Idaho, Montana, and Colorado. And the only payment they accepted were bags of dog food. They had nine K9s—well, ten now with the new puppy, Bear—to feed. One bag of dog food was basically a drop in the bucket of what they went through each week.

She gave Maya and Chase a lot of credit for

holding the family together after her parents went missing. Their Christian faith had gotten them through the dark days, and now many of her siblings were getting married and starting families.

Not that she was planning to head down that path. Especially not after two of her previous boyfriends had cheated on her.

Denali disappeared from her line of sight. Alexis quickened her pace, not wanting the K9 to get too far ahead. As she crested a ridge, she relaxed when she saw Denali sniffing near a bush.

"Break time." K9s needed frequent breaks while working. They expended a lot of energy sniffing their surroundings, and with the hot July sun overhead, she needed to make sure her dog didn't become dehydrated.

Denali lifted her head and bounded toward her. Alexis glanced around, wishing she could get rid of the niggling warning sensation along the back of her neck. Even if someone was out there, she told herself there was nothing to worry about. Stumbling across a fisherman or small game hunter wouldn't be a threat. Alexis took a moment to find a shady spot near some trees and shrugged out of her pack.

In truth, she needed the break more than Denali. Taking her water bottle from the pack, she filled a collapsible bowl for her K9. As Denali lapped at the water, Alexis drained what was left in the bottle.

"Good girl," she praised as Denali stretched out on the ground. "You're doing a great job."

Denali's brown eyes gazed into hers. She leaned forward to hug the dog, then glanced at her watch. They'd been working for an hour, taking a meandering path, and she needed to make sure they could get back to the two-track road where she'd left her SUV.

"We'll go for one more hour, then turn back, okay?" She stroked Denali's soft fur. "I know you won't mind a long nap on our way back to the ranch."

Denali thumped her tail in agreement.

After fifteen minutes, she rose to her feet and offered Denali a little more water. Keeping a dog's mucous membranes moist was key during search and rescue missions. The moisture helped enhance the scent particles, and for cadaver dogs, that was even more important, as the scents were often deeply buried in the ground.

"Search napoo!" She threw her arm wide. "Search!"

Denali eagerly went back to work, trotting along some invisible path that only her dog could smell. Alexis shouldered into her pack and quickly followed. She glanced over her shoulder frequently, but she didn't see anything alarming.

And Denali didn't growl or indicate she noticed anything either.

Alexis was so preoccupied she didn't immediately notice when Denali made an abrupt turn, heading toward a meadow to the east. She nearly tripped over a rock to keep up.

Denali had her nose down and was moving faster now, an indication she may have found something. Remains from one of her parents? Alexis was afraid to hope.

"Search napoo," she said encouragingly. But she needn't have worried. Denali headed to an area, sniffed for long minutes, then sat and let out a sharp bark.

Her alert! Alexis couldn't see much but quickened her pace all the same. Then she abruptly slowed when she realized what Denali had found.

A hand. A badly bloated human hand that had clearly been nibbled on by the local wildlife.

Her stomach twisted painfully as she approached. "Here, Denali," she called. Then she pulled the pink piggy from her backpack. "Good girl! Good girl, Denali!" She tossed the piggy into the air, then cautiously approached the gruesome hand.

Definitely female, she thought, as she crouched

near the spot where it was poking out from the earth. Denali hadn't found her parents' remains as she'd hoped. Based on her experience in other disaster missions, she knew this hand hadn't been there for long. A few days or a week at the most.

She didn't want to disturb what might have been a crime scene. Yet she needed to understand if the hand had been left there by some animal. Or if it was connected to the rest of the body.

Edging as close as she dared, she stared at the bloated hand. That's when she noticed there was a tattoo of flowers encircling the wrist. That reinforced her theory that the hand belonged to a woman.

She took a step back, surveying the area. This area of the earth appeared to have been recently disturbed, but that wasn't conclusive evidence that the rest of the body was buried there. For all she knew, the body had been lying on top of the soil and got dragged away from the area, leaving just the hand behind.

With shaky fingers, she pulled her cell phone from her pack.

No service.

Stifling a sigh, she rummaged for the large, bulky satellite phone Chase had insisted they carry. There had been several cases over the past few months where one of the siblings had been stuck in the mountains without service. The sat phones were nice, but heavy. Within minutes, she heard ringing on the other end of the line.

"Sheriff's office, how may I direct your call?" a female voice asked.

"This is Alexis Sullivan, and my dog has found human remains near—" A crack of gunfire had her stopping abruptly, ducking, and running toward her K9.

She grabbed Denali's vest and pulled the dog into the shelter of the woods. She crouched behind some trees, her heart pounding as she realized she shouldn't have ignored the niggle of warning that had plagued her for the past mile.

The snapping branch had been from a human, not an animal as she'd assumed.

"Hello? Are you there?" the female voice asked from the sat phone.

"I'm here, but someone fired a gun at me. I need police backup!" Even as she said the words, she understood the fruitlessness of her request. Help was hours away at best.

She and Denali were on their own. With a gunman who may be the same person who'd buried the dead body.

"What was that?" FBI Agent Griffin Flannery touched the earpiece attached to his radio. He was just leaving Greybull, Wyoming, but had pulled off to the side of the road when the call came through. "Did I hear Alexis Sullivan call about finding human remains?"

"Yes, and it sounds like someone is firing a gun at her," the dispatcher replied. The radio dispatch channel was open to various law enforcement officials, including the game warden, local police, and those in federal law enforcement.

Like him. His gut churned at the thought of Alexis and Denali being in danger. "What's their location?"

"One moment, please." The dispatcher was silent for a moment, then said, "I can send the coordinates, Griff. She's calling from the southeast portion of the Bighorn Mountains."

"Please do." He quickly executed a U-turn, grateful that he wasn't at his office in Cheyenne when this call came through. "I'm on my way. Are you sending deputies as well?"

"Yes, Deputy Paul Holland has been dispatched to her location," the dispatcher confirmed. "But he's farther out than you are."

"Roger that." Griff didn't have red lights and sirens built into his personal vehicle, but he planted his foot on the gas, going as fast as he dared on the curvy, winding road. "If Alexis calls again, please patch her through to me."

"Right away." The radio connection ended, and Griff focused on navigating the highway. Even with pushing the speed limit, he knew he was a solid thirty to forty minutes away.

If he was a praying man like the Sullivan family, he'd pray for Alexis to be safe. But he and God weren't on speaking terms since he lost his young wife to cancer two years ago. All the prayers in the world hadn't helped save Grace's life.

With a frown, he focused on the brief conversation he'd overheard. Was the body Alexis had found related to the three missing girls he was investigating? They had no indication of foul play, but three missing teenagers had been enough to raise suspicions related to sex trafficking. He was tasked with coordinating a statewide response to the missing teenagers, as they were from different areas of the state. Most recently, a nineteen-year-old by the name of Wendy Evers had been reported missing. He'd been at a small home on the easternmost side of Greybull to interview the nineteen-year-old's grandmother, Barbara Evers, who claimed her granddaughter wouldn't pick up and leave without telling her.

Griff was inclined to believe her.

His radio crackled in his ear. "Griff?"

"Alexis?" He was relieved to hear her voice. "Are you okay?"

"We're fine, but I don't know exactly where the shooter is located." She spoke in a hushed voice, as if she didn't want anyone to overhear. "I had a weird feeling earlier in the search and heard a branch snapping, but I didn't see anything unusual, until now."

"I'm on my way and so is Deputy Paul Holland." He wished he could fly to her side, but calling Logan or one of the other local pilots for a ride would take too long. Hopefully, he'd reach her very soon. "Can you find a place to hide?"

"Yeah, but I don't want to get too far from the site where Denali found the human remains." He heard her murmur reassurances to Denali. "You need to see this, Griff. It looks to me like a recent death. Like within the past week or so."

"What exactly did Denali find?" His intent was to keep her talking. Listening to her voice was reassuring, as if nothing could happen while they were on the phone together. And he'd seen her K9, Denali, in action just a few weeks ago. All the Sullivan K9 teams were impressive when it came to search and rescue missions.

"Just a hand so far. I can't tell you if the rest of the body is buried nearby or not. Unfortunately, the gunman has me pinned down." She sounded frustrated and worried at the same time. "I found some thick foliage, which is helping."

He would have given anything to be there with her right now. He wanted to ask why she was out there alone in the first place but decided against starting an argument. It was a beautiful, warm summer day, no reason Alexis couldn't hike in the mountains with her dog.

Except when that dog happens to find human remains and some idiot decides to fire a gun at her.

"I'll be there soon."

"Okay." Alexis ended the call.

Griff managed to reach the location of Alexis's SUV quickly enough. There was no sign of Holland's sheriff's deputy vehicle, but that was too bad. No way was he waiting around while Alexis hid in the woods from a possible murderer.

Hiking to Alexis's specific location would be the longest part of the trip. He used his compass to double-check his coordinates, then headed into the woods, moving at a light jog. He'd been a runner before he'd had knee surgery and knew he could cover more ground this way. As long as he ignored the pain.

"Alexis? Can you hear me?" He used his radio to connect to her satellite phone.

"Yes, I'm here. Where are you?" Her voice

sounded louder now. "I haven't heard anything for a while, so I think the shooter might be gone."

"Don't take any chances," he warned. "Stay where you are. I'll come to you, okay?"

"Of course, I'll be careful. I would never put Denali at risk." She sounded weary. "But I can't help but wonder if the gunman is related to the hand we found."

He had a bad feeling that was exactly what was going on. "Listen, Alexis, I'm investigating three missing teenage girls. If that guy is connected to that, you need to stay far away."

There was a long moment of silence as she digested that bit of news. "How is it that nobody from the ranch has been called out to search for these girls?"

It was a good question. Griff had learned over the past two years that the Sullivans were often called for missing residents even before law enforcement. Not because the locals were wary of the police, but because the Sullivan family had a stellar reputation. Their skilled K9s had been used to solve many crimes.

He'd participated in several of them recently. He'd been so impressed he'd put in a request to have a K9 of his own. A request that had been promptly denied.

"I'll give you more information on them later,"

he promised. "I happened to be in Greybull following up on the most recent missing girl when your call came through."

"I'm glad you were so close," Alexis said. "I'll be here waiting."

"See you soon." He reluctantly ended the call. He quickened his pace, determined to reach her side sooner rather than later.

If he were honest, he'd admit to having a soft spot for Alexis Sullivan. Not just because she was pretty and smart, although she was both of those things. Compassionate too. No, he was more impressed with her dedication to the Sullivan search and rescue mission.

She was too young for him, though, about six years his junior. And even if she wasn't too young, too sweet, and too good for him, he wasn't interested in opening his heart to love. Not after losing his wife, Grace. He told himself he cared about Alexis and the other Sullivans as friends. They were good people, icons in the community.

Yet he couldn't deny that he'd be devastated if anything happened to Alexis or Denali.

As he ran, he kept a sharp eye out for anything suspicious. He wasn't an expert tracker like Chase Sullivan, but when he passed a spot where what appeared to be a freshly broken branch was lying on the ground, he paused and glanced around. Was this what Alexis had heard? Had the gunman been in this location? Looking up, he noticed the branch had been low enough that it could have been broken by a tall man.

Or someone wielding a rifle.

Telling himself not to be ridiculous, as there were tons of fallen branches lying on the ground, he pushed forward. Yet he'd noticed that most of the other debris on the ground appeared to have been weathered by the elements—the sun, wind, and rain.

Concern for Alexis had him pushing his injured knee to the limit. After what seemed like forever, but was only twenty minutes or so, he checked his coordinates.

He was getting close. Running through the woods had shortened the time it had taken for him to reach Alexis's location. He continued pushing forward, and it was another ten minutes later when he heard a voice call out, "Griff? Is that you?"

"Yes, it's me." He belatedly realized she'd been worried he was the gunman. "I'm roughly sixty yards away."

"I see you," she said. "Denali alerted me that someone was coming."

Thank goodness for her K9, he thought. He knew the border collie wasn't an attack dog, the way her brother Shane's German shepherd, Bryce, was. But he had no doubt the dog would protect her against a threat.

Human or otherwise.

He caught a glimpse of Denali's black and white coat first, then Alexis herself emerged from the trees. He waved at her to stay back, then raised his voice. "FBI! Come out with your hands where I can see them!"

Silence.

Griff hadn't really anticipated the guy would cooperate in turning himself in, but he tried again. "This is Agent Flannery with the FBI! Come out with your hands resting on your head where I can see them!"

More silence. He wanted to believe that meant the guy was long gone, but he wasn't willing to bank his life or Alexis's on that. Still, sometimes alerting the bad guys that he was a federal agent was enough to make them skulk away.

After another long five minutes, he crossed the open meadow to the spot where Alexis and Denali waited in the trees. Thankfully, nobody opened fire on him.

"Hey, Griff." Alexis offered a weak smile. "Fancy meeting you out here."

It surprised him how much he wanted to haul her into his arms. He settled for a grin. "Glad to be of service." Then he sobered. "Where's the human hand you found?"

"This way." Alexis turned and led the way to the other side of the meadow. It took her a few minutes to pinpoint the area, but then she gestured. "It's over there. I tried not to get too close so I wouldn't disturb what could be a crime scene."

"Appreciate that." He glanced over his shoulder, wondering how long it would take for Deputy Paul Holland to get there. Then he carefully approached the clearing. The hand was difficult to see at first because it was bloated and discolored and small lying on the ground.

But as he crept closer, more details became clear. He narrowed his gaze on the splayed fingers. A woman's hand? When he noticed the flowery vine tattoo encircling the wrist, he immediately knew the victim's name.

Not Wendy Evers, as he'd anticipated, but the second missing girl, eighteen-year-old Josie Allen. She'd been reported missing by her place of employment four weeks ago. Josie didn't have any family; she'd moved here from California a year ago, according to the Wooden Hammer bar where she worked.

And Josie had a tattoo just like that in the last photo he had of the young woman. But what didn't make any sense was that Josie had gone missing from Casper, Wyoming. A city that was a solid four-and-a-half- to five-hour drive from this remote location.

Not good. He'd never imagined that he'd find the remains of Josie Allen here in the Bighorn Mountains.

"What do you think?" Alexis asked. "Are the rest of the remains buried there?"

"Yeah, I believe so." He sat back on his heels, looking at the loosely packed ground. He was going to need more than one sheriff's deputy to help him. He'd need a team, including crime scene techs.

But worse than that, Griff grimly realized they weren't dealing with a human trafficking ring, the way he'd originally thought.

This appeared to be the work of a serial killer.

2

____

Alexis stood off to the side with Denali as Griff and Deputy Paul Holland investigated the scene while waiting for additional support to arrive from the medical examiner and crime scene techs. Thankfully, the dispatcher had already put those wheels into motion, so the rest of the team would arrive within the next hour or so.

She made a call of her own to let Anna know she'd be delayed indefinitely because of Denali's find. Anna was their housekeeper and general ranch coordinator, and she promised to let Chase and the other siblings know Alexis was with Griff. The Sullivan K9 Search and Rescue Ranch featured one large ranch house along with ten nice-sized cabins, each with three bedrooms, a bathroom, and a small kitchen. She and her siblings lived in their own places, although recently Chase and his wife, Wynona, and their son, Eli, had moved into the ranch house. Wynona was pregnant, due the following February. Maya was married to Doug Bridges, and they were also expecting, due around Christmas. Maya and Doug were in the process of building an addition to their cabin.

At some point, they would each outgrow their respective homes. Well, except for her since she wasn't interested in dating or settling down. Yet as she watched Griff working, she couldn't help but notice how handsome he was. His light-blond hair was bright in the sun. His expression was serious and intense. At the same time, she'd found him easygoing and not at all arrogant like some federal agents. If things were different . . .

But they weren't. She gave herself a mental shake. There was no point in wishing for something she couldn't have. Even if she was interested in Griffin Flannery, he lived in Cheyenne, which was at least a six-hour drive one way from the ranch.

Considering the guys she'd dated in the past couldn't be faithful while she was out of town for a few weeks working disaster sites, she had no interest in attempting another long-distance relationship.

Besides, Griff was her oldest brother Chase's age, six years older than she was. Granted, he was also more mature than the guys she'd dated, which was a point in his favor.

Whatever. It didn't matter. She debated whether to head back to her SUV for more supplies when Griff crossed toward her.

"Would you mind having Denali search the rest of this area?" Griff glanced at their surroundings. "I'd like to make sure there aren't other dead bodies buried here."

She swallowed hard as the realization of what he was asking sank deep. "You think the other missing girls might be buried nearby?"

"Yes." He nodded toward Denali. "Your K9 will be the one to tell us if that's the case."

"Of course. We'll start right away." She turned and knelt beside Denali. Her K9 had been resting but scrambled to her feet, her tail wagging back and forth with anticipation. "Are you ready, girl? Ready to work?"

She poured water into a collapsible bowl and offered it to Denali. She didn't use a scent source like her siblings did when tracking live people, but the rest of the process was the same. Getting the dog revved up to work was important. They needed to be excited about the job and the ultimate reward. "Search napoo! Search!"

Denali quickly lowered her head and began sniffing the area. Alexis kept the dog away from the location of the swollen hand but still gave the dog room to work. She didn't see anything that could have been a grave, but that didn't mean the bodies hadn't been buried a while ago.

At least since spring, as she assumed the ground would have been too frozen to dig up earlier than that. Especially here in the mountains where the snow took longer to melt.

She followed Denali as her K9 swept the area. She'd trained the dog to use a grid format as preferred in disaster sites. It wasn't always easy to stay on task with obstacles like trees and rocks getting in the way, but they managed.

Alexis was torn between hoping Denali found something and praying she didn't. Griff hadn't filled her in on the details of the three missing girls, other than to say this one matched the description of one girl, and she wanted to believe the other two were still alive.

Yet if they were dead, she wanted to find them so their families could lay them to rest in a proper burial.

"Search napoo," she repeated encouragingly. They were almost a hundred yards from the initial burial site when Denali abruptly stopped, sniffed for long moments, then sat and barked.

Her alert! She was about to call out to Griff, but

he must have been trailing behind them because he rushed forward. "What did she find?"

"I'm not sure." There were no obvious body parts sticking out the way the hand had been. Alexis moved closer to examine the ground. It seemed harder packed than the area where the hand was sticking out. She glanced back at Griff. "Looks like we might need to dig a bit to see what's down there."

"Could it be a dead animal?" Griff asked.

"No, Denali is able to differentiate between animal decay and people." She smiled grimly. "People smell different to dogs, or so I'm told. Denali has never alerted on anything but human remains."

"Okay, that's good enough for me." He sighed and glanced back to where Paul was standing near the initial burial site. "I'll grab Paul's shovel."

She nodded and took a moment to reward Denali. When she tossed the piggy up into the air, her K9 leaped up to snatch it. Then Denali lowered into a playful stance, lowering her front legs, leaving her hind end up, tail wagging with excitement. This was always the hardest part for Alexis. The K9 deserved to be rewarded for a job well done, but finding a dead body was never a fun thing.

Yet this was the work she'd chosen, so she did her best to put the apprehension behind her. Griff returned with a shovel and quickly stabbed the point of the blade into the dirt.

"What if you hit the body?" she asked. "Shouldn't we use something smaller?"

"This isn't optimal," he agreed. "But I need to know what we're dealing with." Griff leaned on the shovel and removed the dirt. She peered down at the opening but didn't see anything.

Griff dug a small trench around the area where Denali alerted. Sweat rolled down the sides of his face, darkening his shirt under his arms, but he kept going, determined to uncover whatever Denali had scented. Another five minutes passed, but then he set the shovel aside and dropped to his knees. "I found something."

Her stomach clenched as she crouched beside him. Then nausea swirled as she realized they were looking at a young woman's head—the face was still partially covered in dirt, but there was plenty of matted hair. She abruptly stood and stumbled back, trying not to throw up.

"I think this is the first victim, Megan Riley," Griff said in a low voice. "She had long dark hair."

Alexis could only nod, still fighting the urge to lose her breakfast. She took several deep breaths through her mouth, struggling to maintain control. "You mentioned three missing girls? And we've found two of them?"

"Yes." He rose and crossed over to where she stood. "I believe we've found Josie Allen and Megan

Riley. The third girl, Wendy Evers, hasn't been missing for long, but if you wouldn't mind asking Denali to keep searching, that would be great." He frowned and raked his gaze over the area. "The killer must have realized you were getting too close to where he'd left the bodies, and that's why he fired at you."

The thought of being out in the wilderness with a killer was horrifying. "I wish I could have gotten a good look at him."

Griff sent her a sharp look. "I'm glad you're not hurt. When I think of how long it took me to get here…"

"I think you're right about his intent to scare me off. And I'm fine, Griff." She turned toward her K9. "Here, Denali. Hand."

The dog dropped the piggy into her outstretched palm. Alexis tucked it away, then bent to smooth her hands over the dog's furry pelt. There were some prickers embedded in the black and white coat, and she took a moment to pull them free. Then she offered her K9 more water. When the dog was satiated, she rose to her feet.

"Napoo! Search napoo!"

Denali seemed to understand she needed to find napoo in another area, so she moved away from the most recent find. This was how it worked at disaster sites too. The dogs intuitively knew there was more work to do and moved onto the next area to search.

As she followed Denali, Alexis couldn't help thinking about the killer lurking nearby. She didn't think he was still close, but what if he was? She could easily imagine him sitting high up somewhere, watching them through a rifle scope or binoculars.

What kind of man callously killed young girls? *A sick one*, she decided. A horribly sick man who didn't value life.

Like the devil himself.

Someone called out, and she turned to see that the rest of the crime scene team had arrived. Griff hurried over to meet with the newcomers, no doubt filling them in on the most recent find.

She and Denali worked the area for a full hour with two rest breaks. Denali alerted on what appeared to be a small bone fragment. She wasn't an expert, but she thought the bone could be part of a forearm. She showed it to Griff.

"Denali found this."

He frowned. "Wendy hasn't been gone long enough for this to belong to her."

"Yeah, I know." She turned the bone in her fingers. Did it come from her parents? Or maybe the pilot? She knew it wasn't likely. An animal could have moved the bone fragment from one place to the other. The only way to know for sure was to have it tested for DNA. A process that would take weeks, if not months. She tucked it away to show Chase and Maya. She looked at Griff. "I don't think there's anyone else here. We've checked the entire field. I don't see this guy burying a girl in the woods."

He nodded. "I doubt that too. Thanks for trying. Hopefully, this means the most recent victim is still alive."

She shivered despite the hot July sun. Even if the most recent victim, Wendy Evers, was still alive, she didn't want to imagine what she might be suffering through while knowing how the torture would end.

With her death.

GRIFF STILL NEEDED solid confirmation that Alexis and Denali had uncovered the first two missing girls, he couldn't simply base his suspicions on a tattoo similar to Josie Allen's and a woman with dark hair like Megan Riley, but his gut told him they were standing in the middle of the serial killer's burial ground.

Two victims so far, not three. But he was plagued by a sense of urgency to find Wendy Evers before it was too late.

He scanned the horizon, wondering if the guy was still out there. Doubtful, but as soon as more officers arrived on scene, he'd spread out to do a search.

And that gave him an idea.

"Alexis? Can Shane come out with Bryce to track the killer?" He kicked himself for not thinking of the possibility sooner. Then he hastily added, "Or one of the other Sullivans, whoever is available?"

"Everyone has been tied up with other cases, that's why I decided to work alone today." She shrugged. "I know Shane is in Laramie. Let me try Joel, he was helping someone local." Alexis pulled out her phone, sighed, then tucked it away. "I'll have to use the sat phone as this is a dead zone."

Dead being the operative word, he thought grimly.

She rummaged in her backpack for the bulky sat phone. He listened as she made the call, giving the same detailed coordinates she'd provided for him. When she finished, she turned to face him. "Joel and his K9, Royal, will be here soon. Sounds like Logan just finished a charter and is willing to drop Joel and Royal off nearby." She put a hand to her stomach. "They're bringing food, too, not that I'm in the mood to eat."

He wasn't hungry either. Finding dead bodies tended to ruin a man's appetite. Still, others may be interested in lunch. "That's great news. I wish I had thought of it sooner."

"Probably wouldn't have mattered." Alexis grimaced. "Summer is our busiest time of the year, and the siblings have been spread out across the country. I'm glad Joel and Royal got back in time to help."

He nodded. "That's good for us. Although from what I remember, Royal isn't an attack dog like Bryce."

The corner of her mouth tipped up in a smile. "No, but you'd be surprised. Royal might be a sweet black lab who is anxious to please, but he can be fierce if needed." She glanced at Denali, and added, "All of our dogs can be protective in the face of a threat. Besides, Royal is a great tracker."

Since he sensed that was true, he let it go. Although deep down, he knew this guy they were after was a vicious killer.

But considering the way he'd fired at Alexis from a safe distance, he might also be a coward. They'd know when they found him.

"What do you know about Wendy Evers?" Alexis asked.

"She's nineteen and has been missing for two days." *Two long days*, he thought somberly. "Her grandmother reported her missing late last night. I drove up from Cheyenne first thing this morning to interview her. Wendy works in a pub in Greybull.

Two of the three victims worked at bars, but all in different cities. Josie Allen disappeared after working her shift at a bar in Casper, which as you know is a long way from here. Megan Riley is from Jackson." He shook his head, battling a wave of frustration. "I don't know how this guy is choosing his victims or why he's traveling hundreds of miles to find them. Maybe he's a trucker? Or has a job that requires a lot of travel?"

"I'm no expert, but what bothers me is that this guy might be escalating," Alexis said thoughtfully. "Maybe he buried Josie here a week ago and then felt compelled to find the next girl sooner than usual." Her blue eyes held his. "That could be why he grabbed her from a closer city like Greybull."

It was a good point. One that made him feel as if they may already be too late to save Wendy Evers. Not that he'd stop trying to find her. "I'll need to talk to some of my FBI colleagues." Griff frowned. "Now that we have two dead girls, I need one of their profilers to get involved."

"Agent Flannery!" He turned to glance over to where the crime scene techs were gathered around the gravesite where Denali had found the bloated hand. He quickly crossed over to join them.

"I told you, call me Griff." Nobody in Wyoming used formal titles. When he glanced at down at the uncovered grave, his stomach clenched. The victim was a teenage girl; her face was bloated, and there were dark ligature marks around her neck. Still, he easily recognized Josie Allen. "Looks like she may have been strangled."

"I would agree with that assessment, but we'll need the ME to tell us for sure," the deputy agreed. It was a cop Griff had never met, but his name tag identified his last name as Gordon. "There's no ID on her body."

Griff pulled out his phone. There was no cell service, but he was able to access his pictures. He thumbed through to find Josie and showed the image to Deputy Gordon. "I'm fairly certain the body is that of Josie Allen. Reported missing from Casper, Wyoming, ten days ago."

"Casper, huh?" The deputy shook his head. "She's a long way from there."

He nodded, then waved behind them. "Alexis and Denali found another body about two hundred yards from here. Very possibly the first missing girl, Megan Riley."

Gordon whistled. "That's not good."

No, it wasn't. He turned to where the crime scene techs were standing off to the side, giving the ME room to work. "Will you both come with me? We found another victim."

The pair of techs glanced at each other with concern. "You're saying this guy is a serial killer?"

"It sure looks that way." Griff knew it was only a matter of time before the news of a madman targeting young girls traveled across the state. A discovery like this would bring in the national media, too, something he was not looking forward to. That level of attention was exactly what this guy wanted.

And it would make his already difficult job that much harder. But there wasn't anything he could do other than keep working the case.

"This way." He gestured for them to follow. "I'll show you."

The techs hurried after him, bringing their box of tools. They had smaller trowels, brushes, and mini rakes to help expose a buried corpse. He didn't believe this area was the actual location where the girls had been murdered. Having a third missing girl made him think the killer was keeping the victims in a van, cabin, or some other location where he could kill the girls without being seen or heard. Then he brought them there to bury them.

Did that mean his home was nearby? Some serial killers wanted to be near the location where they left their victims so they could visit and relive their kill. Although in this case, Alexis was right that the guy had quickly turned his attention to another victim.

The techs went to work, carefully removing the packed dirt from around the dead body. This one took more time as the body had been there longer. Megan had been reported missing a month ago from Jackson. She hadn't worked in a bar like the others, but at a grocery store. If Megan was the first victim, it could be that the guy chose her on impulse.

Yet he couldn't say for sure there wasn't another missing girl somewhere. Maybe a victim who didn't have friends or family to report her as missing. Griff had planned to scour the missing children database to see if there were other likely victims out there, but he hadn't had time yet. Another reason to get additional resources here from Washington, DC, or maybe the field office in Denver or Phoenix.

He borrowed Alexis's sat phone to make the call to his boss, who promised to relay the information up the chain of command.

"Griff? You want to come check this out?" Suzanne, the female crime scene tech, called him over.

He returned to the grave and slowly nodded. "Yes, that looks like Megan Riley. And like the other victim, she's been strangled too." He sighed and raked his fingers through his hair. "Two of three victims have been found. We really need to figure out who this guy is in time to save Wendy Evers."

"We'll ask the ME to come take a look here when he's finished with the first victim," Zack Hart, the second crime scene tech, said. He stared down at the dead woman. "I don't like knowing this guy is out there walking the streets in our cities."

Griff understood the tech's concern. He didn't much like it either. Before he could say anything more, though, he heard the rumble of a plane engine. Shielding his eyes against the sun, he watched as the small prop plane belonging to Logan Fletcher banked in a curve, likely looking for a place to land.

The mountain region didn't offer much as far as plane landing sites. They'd likely have to use the two-track road back where they left their vehicles.

"Alexis, do you want to come with me to meet your brother?" He gestured to the second grave. "There's nothing more we can do here."

"Sure." Alexis looked relieved at the thought of moving away from the gruesome finds. He'd heard she and Denali worked several disaster sites over the past year, but he was convinced that finding brutally murdered teenagers was different.

He stopped briefly to chat with the ME, then used his compass to retrace his path back to the two-track road. Alexis and Denali fell into step beside him.

"I hope we'll be able to find a trace of this guy," Alexis said. "It's not like we have a great scent source to work from. Joel's K9, Royal, might be able to hit on the scent near the graves, but there's no guarantee."

"We may have another source," he said. "I passed what could have been the broken branch you heard." He shrugged. "It's worth a try."

"That could work. Especially if Royal can pick up the scent from both the branch and the grave sites." She looked up at the trees overhead. "We should count our blessings. We have good weather and plenty of daylight."

He grunted without saying anything. Two girls were dead, and one was in grave danger. There were no blessings here that he could see.

When they reached the fallen branch, he pointed at the tree trunk where it had broken off. "I'm thinking he accidentally hit it with his rifle. Maybe it was sticking out of a backpack or something."

"Yes. Joel would know better than I would, but it looks recent." She grimaced. "I'm not a hunter the way Joel, Shane, Chase, and the others are."

"I understand." Griff had been deer and elk hunting, but he generally preferred fishing. Not that he was able to get out of Cheyenne as much as he'd like to enjoy the outdoors.

The Sullivans were a magnet for trouble, he thought as they continued on. Five minutes later, they met Logan, Jessica with her K9, Teddy, Joel, and his K9, Royal.

"I didn't know Jess and Teddy were tagging along," Alexis said.

"No reason you guys should have all the fun." Jessica strove for a light tone, but her expression was one of concern. "Besides, from what I've heard, we need all the help we can get to bring this guy to justice."

"Agreed," Griff said. "Okay, let's head back this way to what will hopefully be our starting point."

The broken branch wasn't much to go on, but Griff didn't have a lot of other options. He watched as both Teddy and Royal sniffed the ground with interest. Griff had faith in both dogs, especially Royal, as he'd seen the black lab in action. Jessica's Teddy was a narcotics dog, cross-trained to find people as well.

After both dogs had been given water, Joel and Jess instructed them to search for the bad guy.

Both K9s put their noses to the ground and headed in the general direction of the burial site. Griff was encouraged, though, when Royal and Teddy veered off the path to the north.

He glanced at Alexis, who nodded thoughtfully. "I think they're following his trail."

"Really?" He was almost afraid to hope. Rather than taking a direct route back to the dead bodies, he and Alexis followed Joel and Jessica in a wide arc. After thirty minutes of walking, though, the Sullivans called for a break.

"It's hot, and the dogs are panting quite a bit," Joel explained. "That's how they sweat, but it's also an indication that they need a rest."

"I understand." There was no point in complaining. He appreciated how the Sullivans treated their dogs with care and concern.

"I brought snacks." Logan rummaged through his pack. "Plenty of water, protein bars, and dried fruit."

Griff wasn't that hungry, but he knew it was smart to eat. Logan passed along the goodies, and even Alexis accepted a protein bar and water.

"What's this about the guy shooting at Alexis?" Joel asked.

She wrinkled her nose. "He missed. And I'm sure he was trying to get me away from the location of the dead girls."

"Good thing he missed," Jessica muttered. "Chase would not be happy if something bad happened to you. You know he hates it when we work alone."

Griff knew Chase had worked a case alone back in February, but that situation had been different. Sort of.

They rested without saying much for ten minutes, then Joel pushed himself up from the ground. "Time to get moving."

Griff's knee was killing him, but he did his best to ignore the pain. The Sullivans went through the routine of offering their dogs water and telling them to search the bad guy. As before, both dogs quickly went to work.

It was less than ten minutes later when they reached a hill that had a direct line of sight to the activity around the graves. Then Royal let out a sharp bark.

Griff turned to glance at Joel. "What did he find?"

"A shell casing." Joel gestured to the hint of brass lying partially beneath the leaves. "Looks to be from a rifle."

"Really?" Griff hurried over to see for himself. Then he used an evidence bag as a glove to pick it up. The shell casing alone wasn't proof of anything, as the woods teemed with hunters during the peak hunting season.

But considering the direct line of sight to the grave sites, Griff felt certain the shell casing had been fired by the killer.

3

Alexis shivered despite the hot July sun beating down on them. The location of the shell casing indicated the serial killer was standing there when he'd taken a shot at her.

Turning, she looked back at the graves. There was a clear line of sight, so she wasn't sure how this guy hadn't hit her or Denali.

As if reading her thoughts, Griff scowled. "Either he's not a good shot or the sun was too bright. We're facing east, and Alexis is wearing green. Maybe he hadn't been able to see her clearly because of the foliage nearby."

"Maybe," her brother Joel admitted. "But if he's a hunter, he should have hit his target."

"Gee, thanks," Alexis muttered. "I'm glad he

didn't, but I'm sure he was just trying to scare me off."

"There's that." Griff nodded in agreement. "If this is our suspect, he likes to kill his victims up close and personal."

That observation did not make her feel any better. She'd seen the ligature marks around the victims' throats. She hated to imagine the last image those girls had seen was an evil man's face looming over them. Swallowing hard, she turned to Joel and Jess. "Let's keep following his trail. Maybe he owns a place nearby."

Her siblings glanced at each other, then nodded. "After we take a quick break," Jessica said. "The dogs are hot."

"I understand." She knew Denali was getting tired too.

Griff stared down at the shell casing in the evidence bag. "Hopefully, the lab can do something with this."

"Prints?" Alexis asked. "I doubt this guy was wearing gloves in the middle of summer."

"That's my hope," Griff said. "Although I'm not sure this guy is in the system."

She sighed. The trees offered plenty of shade. They sat beneath them on the ground with the dogs to rest.

"You have no idea who this guy is?" Jessica asked Griff.

"Not yet." Griff frowned. "But we need to find him soon. I'm hoping he lives here in the area."

"Tell us about Wendy Evers," Alexis suggested. "Do you have a picture of her?"

"Yes." Griff pulled out his phone and swiped at the screen. Then he passed it to her. "She's blond and has a nose piercing. The three girls don't look anything alike, other than being in their late teens or early twenties, so he's not picking them based on a type."

She gazed at Wendy Evers's smiling face, feeling slightly sick to her stomach. Then she passed the phone to Joel. He winced, then passed the device to Jessica who also looked somber before she handed it to her husband, Logan.

"Her grandmother claims Wendy wouldn't have left without telling her. I guess Wendy lives on her own, but she and her grandmother are close." Griff tucked the phone back into his pocket. "The other two women were also single and lived alone. I think that may be something he looks for in a victim. But it's gnawing at me that we don't know what made him decide to pick these specific girls in three different cities across the state."

There was a long silence as they digested that bit of information.

"We'll find him," Joel said with confidence. Then he jumped to his feet. "Let's go. The dogs should be able to follow the scent trail since he was here recently."

Alexis agreed. The three of them went through the routine of offering water to the dogs, then revving them up for the search.

Joel's Royal took the lead with Jess and Teddy close at his side. She and Griff and Denali were last. Yet as they walked, it was obvious that both dogs were hot on the same scent.

"I can't get over how well they track people." Griff shook his head, his green gaze full of admiration. "They're amazing."

"Yes." She bent to smooth her hand over Denali's soft fur. "We're very blessed."

He nodded without saying anything. She didn't know if Griff was a believer. They'd worked together before, and he always participated in before-meal prayers, but he also didn't say much about his faith.

She wanted to ask but was distracted by the sound of rushing water. "Is that a river?"

"Up ahead," Joel said. "More of a creek, but it's deep enough that we're going to let the dogs cool off in the water."

"Good idea." She knew Denali would love to splash in the water.

They quickened their pace, still following the

scent trail. Ironically, Royal reached the stream first. He let out a sharp bark, then sat, staring back at Joel.

"Good boy." Joel pulled the stuffed beaver from his pocket. He tossed it for Royal, who leaped up to catch it. Royal ran in a circle with the brown beaver in his mouth, then he dropped it to jump into the stream. Without hesitation, Teddy and Denali jumped in behind him. The current wasn't brisk enough to worry about. That was more of an issue in the spring when the thick layer of snow began to melt. Usually by July, the water level was lower.

"Wait, let me look for footprints," Griff said, holding up a hand to keep Joel from going any closer.

Her brother nodded and crouched to peer at the ground. Griff did too.

"I don't see anything," Joel said.

"Me either." Griff grimaced as he stood. He bent to massage his left knee, making Alexis frown. Was he hurt? If so, he shouldn't be hiking in the mountains. When he noticed her looking at him, Griff dropped his hand and gestured to the river. "Looks like the dogs have the right idea."

"They do." Jess dropped to her knees. "The water is nice and cold."

Jess used her cupped hands to splash water on

her face. Alexis joined her. And soon the guys were crouched at the bank too.

"We know our perp was here." Griff wiped the water from his face and rose to his feet to look around the area. "I wish we could have found boot prints."

"We'll keep the dogs on his scent." Joel grinned as Royal splashed through the stream. "Cooling them down will help."

Alexis looked for familiar landmarks but didn't see any. They had been heading in a general western direction, which in theory would eventually lead to the area where she'd left her SUV and the others likely had too.

"Come, Denali." Alexis didn't bother to try to avoid the droplets that pelted her when Denali shook herself to get rid of the excess water. "Good girl."

Joel and Jess called their respective K9s too and were subject to the same drenching. In truth, the cold water felt good. Soon, Joel and Jess had their dogs back on the scent. Alexis wasn't surprised when the dogs followed the stream.

She wasn't sure how they'd followed the scent, other than the shooter must have been sweating to the point that some of those particles hit the earth near the stream. Often people purposefully walked through water to avoid leaving a trail.

And this guy must have known something about that strategy to have tried it here. Thankfully, July was hot enough to work in their favor.

They walked in silence. Joel and Jess kept an eye on their dogs while the rest of them followed. After about twenty minutes, Royal abruptly stopped, turned, and walked through the creek to the other side.

Jessica's Teddy did the same thing.

"Our guy got out of the stream here?" Griff hurried ahead to peer at the water's edge. "I don't see footprints, but the ground is damp here."

Alexis eyed her watch. "It's been several hours since he took that shot." She shrugged, then added, "I'm surprised the sun hasn't dried it up completely by now."

"Yeah. Good point." Griff stood for a moment with his hands on his hips. "It makes me wonder if he stayed back at the location where we found the shell casing for a while. Maybe watching you, Alexis."

"Maybe." The last thing she wanted was to capture the attention of a serial killer. Griff had mentioned he wasn't sure how this guy was choosing his victims, other than they were young and lived alone.

She didn't live alone, considering there were nine other cabins on the ranch housing her siblings. And nobody could get on the ranch without at least one of the dogs, and more likely all of them, raising the alarm.

"I don't think you should go anywhere alone, Alexis," Griff said in a low voice. "Not until we get this guy."

She arched a brow. "Just me? Or all young women who might be targeted by this sick guy?"

"All women, yes"—Griff held her gaze for a long moment—"but especially you. He likely watched you from afar, the way he must have observed his earlier victims before making his move." Griff reached for her hand. "Promise me you'll be careful."

"I promise." She couldn't deny being disturbed over the idea of this guy becoming obsessed with her. The one good thing was that she never went anywhere without Denali at her side.

If this guy tried anything, he'd be in for a rude awakening. Denali might look harmless, but the K9 would protect Alexis from a threat.

She only hoped it wouldn't come to that.

GRIFF WAS TIRED, sore, and hungry. But, of course, he didn't complain. With the Sullivan K9s following the scent trail, he had no intention of stopping. The stream was well behind them now, as the dogs continued moving southwest.

His phone rang, catching him off guard. They must have reached a location with cell service. He ducked under a low-hanging branch as he reached for his phone. Seeing his boss's name on the screen, he quickly answered. "This is Flannery."

"Did you find anything more?" His boss was Special Agent in Charge Holden Ring. He was originally from Texas, and the other agents who reported to him secretly called him Tex.

Griff suppressed a sigh. His boss was all about looking good to the upper brass. Tex wanted nothing more than to be promoted within the bureau. Griff liked his post in Cheyenne, which was generally considered a bottom-of-the-barrel assignment. "Not much. The two victims that were found with the help of Denali, one of the Sullivan K9s, are being taken to Greybull where the medical examiner will perform full autopsies. They appear to have been strangled, and both of them were wearing clothes, which tells me if he sexually assaulted them, he took the time to put their clothes back on."

"That would be unusual," Holden, a.k.a. Tex, admitted. "I'd like those autopsy reports ASAP."

Griff rolled his eyes since Tex couldn't see him. After a moment, he decided to come clean about the shell casing. "Royal is another Sullivan K9. He found a shell casing. Someone shot at Alexis Sullivan, and we think it could be our guy. I'll send that to the lab as soon as we get off the mountain."

"That's good work," Tex said. And since compliments were rare, Griff knew his boss would use that information to assure the higher ups they were close to nailing this guy. "I need you to keep me in the loop."

"You know as well as I do there isn't cell service in the mountains." Griff kept his tone reasonable, although he was irritated at knowing his boss would be hounding his every move throughout the investigation. "I just now got into range. What about that profiler I requested?"

"Yes, a woman named Cheri Artez will be flying into Cheyenne."

"Have her fly into Yellowstone," Griff said. "Cheyenne is too far away. I'm not leaving to pick her up. She can either change her flight in Denver or drive up herself from Cheyenne." He was annoyed all over again. Tex never seemed to appreciate Wyoming being vast and rural, despite having come from a similar state.

"Okay, I'll let her know." There was a pause, then Tex added, "Artez is young and relatively new in her role."

Griff ground his teeth. He knew that if he was in

LA or Chicago, he'd get someone higher up the chain to help. Instead, he was saddled with a rookie.

As if reading his silence, his boss added, "I hear she's good. Knows her stuff. Did some great work on a case in Orlando earlier this year. She's heading out first thing in the morning."

Griff sighed. What could he do? A rookie was better than no one. "Okay, give her my cell number. She can call me when she gets in the area."

"Will do. Don't forget to keep me informed," Tex reiterated. "It's only a matter of time before the press gets wind of this."

"I know. Thanks." Griff ended the call. Feeling Alexis's gaze, he forced a smile. "The FBI is sending a profiler out to help us. She'll be here tomorrow morning."

Alexis nodded. "I heard."

He didn't want to air his grievances with the bureaucracy with her. Most of the local people here didn't appreciate having the federal government poking its nose in their business. Most of the frustration was with the EPA and the DNR. But the FBI wasn't well loved either.

Until they were needed, as in a case like this.

Griff had to admit the Sullivan family had always treated him kindly and with respect. There was none of the avoidance some of the other residents had shown over the course of his career.

During the first year after his wife's death, Griff had walked around in a fog without even noticing the hard stares. It was only after some of that grief faded that he'd understood how many people wished he'd get lost.

Pushing that aside, he focused on the dogs. It didn't take long for him to recognize their surroundings.

"Are we close to the campground?" Griff asked.

"I believe so." Jess elbowed Logan. "We know this area well, don't we?"

"Yep." Logan gestured to a bat house mounted in a tree up ahead. "A few years ago, one of the campers put that up to help keep the mosquito population at bay."

"It does look familiar," Joel agreed. "We'll need to take another break soon, though. Royal is getting tired."

"Teddy is too." Jessica frowned. "Both dogs have black coats, which makes searching in the summer more difficult."

Alexis glanced at Griff, expecting him to be frustrated at the delay. Instead, he looked relieved. "Works for me."

Joel headed to a grove of trees offering a plethora of shade. They shrugged out of their packs and sat with their backs up against a tree. Griff massaged his left knee. She frowned and gestured to it. "What happened? Did you injure it recently?"

He sighed, but this time, he didn't stop kneading the joint. "Knee surgery back in January. I tore my ACL and needed surgery to repair it."

"Ouch." Her gaze was sympathetic. "Playing basketball?"

"I usually run, but this happened when I was skiing in Jackson." One of his few ski trips over the winter. "I may have started running again too soon, though. I should have waited."

She grinned. "You? Impatient? Go figure."

"You and the rest of your siblings seem to have the patience of a saint," he said. "Except maybe for Chase."

Joel barked out a laugh. "You got that right. Chase is more like his K9 Rocky than he cares to admit."

"We have to be patient when it comes to the dogs," Alexis said. "They're great at their jobs, but they can't be rushed."

"I see that." Griff wondered if he'd have the patience to handle a K9. Logan handed out more snacks, and he offered a piece of his protein bar to Denali. The beautiful collie simply cocked her head without making any effort to take the morsel.

"We don't give our dogs table food." Alexis

shook her head for emphasis. "And our dogs are trained not to take food from anyone but us."

"It's for their safety," Jessica added. "Some people might try to harm a dog or shake the K9 from their scent trail by leaving poisoned or bad food out. Our dogs will sniff at it, but they won't eat."

Griff hated the idea of someone purposefully harming a dog. "Sorry. I should have known." He popped the piece of protein bar into his own mouth. "You'll have to tell me what brand of dog food you need. I'm not sure where this trail ends, but I'll likely need your services again."

"Don't worry about it." Alexis waved a hand. "This is different. We're the ones who stumbled across the first dead body."

He knew the shooter hadn't anticipated that Alexis and her cadaver dog, Denali, would come across his burial site. "Yeah, well, the government should reimburse you. Especially since my boss denied my request to get a K9 of my own."

"You asked for one?" Alexis asked in surprise.

"Yep. But my boss said"—he used his fingers to make air quotes—"'That's not in the budget.'"

"In his defense, having K9s isn't cheap," Jess said. "Training is a huge initial investment, but even after that, food, vet bills, and gear. It all adds up."

"Dogs need a lot of attention," Alexis said. "Beyond the initial training, we're always working with our K9s to keep them interested in playing the search game."

"Thankfully, the dogs are much like four-year-olds who can play the same game over and over and over again," Joel joked. "It's crazy-making."

"Okay, you're right. I probably didn't think it through." He stroked a hand over Denali's fur. His job required him to travel around the state, which made it difficult to have a dog as a pet.

Joel pulled an old topographical map from his backpack. After studying it for a few minutes, he nodded. "We're only a mile or so from the campground." He glanced at Griff. "That's not where you and Alexis left your SUVs, is it?"

"No. They're farther south." He nodded at Alexis. "I followed her lead."

"I chose the search area based on the plane piece you and Logan found back in April," Alexis said. "I moved a few miles away, though, to search a new area we haven't been to yet."

"I landed the plane in the same area we used back then," Logan said. "It's not that far from here."

"Okay." Griff hid a wince as he rose to his feet. "I think we need to follow this guy's trail until it ends. From there, you can head home." He glanced at Alexis, including her in that plan. "Thanks for your help, but there's nothing more that you and Denali can do. I'd feel better if you would head home with the rest of your siblings."

She frowned but didn't argue. He was relieved she'd planned to uphold her promise not to head out alone.

"Royal and I can drive back with you," Joel offered. "Jess and Logan can fly back via the plane."

"Sure." Alexis sighed. "I guess I can cross that section off the list as far as searching for our parents. Well, except for the bone I found."

"What bone?" Jess asked.

"It's probably nothing." Alexis patted the pack. "I'll have you guys take it back with you to be tested."

"That's interesting." Jessica's gaze turned thoughtful. "I guess it can't hurt to check it out."

The Sullivan siblings got their dogs ready to go. Moments later, Royal and Teddy were back on the scent trail. Griff was surprised even Denali seemed to be sniffing the same areas as the other dogs.

As he and Alexis followed the others, he nodded at Denali. "Can she track live people?"

"That's not her specialty, but she can." Alexis shrugged, glancing at him. "When we worked the tornado scene in North Carolina, Denali found both live and dead victims."

"Interesting." He hoped that meant Denali would alert if this guy got anywhere near Alexis. He was glad she'd be on the ranch with her siblings close at hand.

Fifteen minutes later, he could see the campground. The place was packed with tents, small campers, and even larger campers. There was so much activity, he wondered if any of the visitors had seen the killer.

But it soon became apparent that the scent trail circumvented the campground itself. Royal and Teddy led them in a roundabout path toward the parking lot.

And that's where the scent trail ended.

"This is it," Joel said as Royal sat and let out a sharp bark. "This guy must have left his vehicle in this spot."

Griff scanned the asphalt and noted a couple of small oil spots. It wasn't much, but as he squatted beside them, he could see they were fresh.

"Our guy drives a vehicle that leaks oil." He sighed, rising to his feet. "I guess that's something."

The parking lot was three-quarters of the way full, but there was nobody around now. He figured most of the cars belonged to those staying in tents.

"I'm sorry." Alexis touched his arm. "I know this doesn't give you anything to go on."

"Not your fault." He forced a smile. "I know more about our perp now than I did when I set out this morning." He thought of the shell casing and pulled the evidence bag from his pocket, glancing at Logan. "I don't suppose you'd be willing to fly this to Cheyenne tomorrow to drop this at the evidence lab?"

"I'd be glad to," Logan agreed.

"Thanks." The bag had a label, so he signed it and then had Logan do the same. "Have the lab call me if they lift a print."

"Will do." Logan pocketed the bag and glanced at his wife. "Ready to go?"

"Wait, I don't want to forget the bone either." Alexis dug in her pack. "Ask Chase and Doug if we can get it tested for DNA."

"It would be amazing if it belonged to our parents," Jess said.

"That or the pilot." Alexis shrugged. "Or none of them. Like I said, it's a long shot."

Nodding, Jessica pocketed the fragment. "Okay, we'll see you back at the ranch."

Joel and Royal stayed back. Griff glanced at Alexis. "Are you ready to head back to our SUVs?"

"Yep." Alexis had her compass out. "We're going to backtrack a bit, but they're closer than the plane."

He agreed with her assessment. Joel and Royal were a few feet away, playing with Royal's stuffed beaver. The dog had alerted after all.

They turned to head back into the woods. Alexis and Denali took the lead. Griff stayed close behind her, leaving Joel and Royal to follow them. Joel didn't know the location of the SUVs as he'd come via the plane.

To Griff's surprise and supreme gratitude, the hike didn't take as long as he had feared. The roads out here took many twists and turns, going around extremely large trees and fallen rocks. When they reached the road, he realized it was an offshoot of the one leading to the campground.

He'd been in such a hurry, he hadn't noticed before.

"The car is up ahead," Alexis called. Then she frowned. "Hey, Denali, where are you going?" The dog had begun to growl.

Alexis veered to the right to follow her K9 just as a crack of gunfire rang out.

"Down, get down!" Griff shouted as he threw himself toward Alexis who in turn was covering Denali with her body while trying to get the dog to safety behind a nearby tree.

"Where's the shooter?" Joel asked.

It was a good question. And Griff had no doubt in his mind the serial killer had found Alexis's vehicle and had waited for the opportunity to attack.

The earlier shooting may have been a warning, but not this one.

This time, Griff knew the guy had intended to take Alexis out of the picture, permanently.

4

———————

Where was the shooter? Sandwiched between Griff and Denali, she couldn't see much beyond the tree she'd used as cover. She knew her brother Joel and Royal were nearby, too, not that she could see them either.

The twelve-inch-wide trunk wasn't enough coverage. If this guy had a scope on that rifle of his, he could easily kill her and Griff.

Maybe with one shot.

Her stomach knotted as she realized this guy had come there to wait for her. She had put the people she cared about and her dog in danger.

Griff pushed her closer to the ground. "Stay down." Then he took aim and fired. She had no idea if he could see the killer or not. The gunfire was deafening. She wondered if any of the campers nearby would run over.

No, they'd more likely run away from the sound. Or assume it was a hunter. Not that July was hunting season.

A second shot rang out. At first, her pulse spiked in alarm, until she realized Joel had joined the fight. She understood Griff and Joel were trying to warn the killer that there were two of them who were armed.

She prayed their plan would work. As the ringing in her ears faded, a heavy silence hung over the area. Seconds ticked off in her mind. She could barely see the wheels of her SUV. Or Griff's. Hard to say for sure.

"Is he gone?" She spoke in a hushed whisper. Denali remained remarkably calm, despite the gunfire. That was due to Maya and Chase who had insisted they train their dogs while other members of the family were doing target practice at their firing range.

"I'm not sure." Griff's voice was low and grim. "I'd like to know how he found your vehicle."

She frowned. Her car did not have the Sullivan K9 Search and Rescue logo stenciled along the side. The logo had been Chase's idea, but after Maya was targeted back in January, her brother had realized announcing who they were to the world was a mistake. Over the past six months, the entire fleet of SUVs had been repainted in basic black. "I have no idea. My car does have the crate area for Denali, but how would he even know to look here?"

"I don't know." Griff shifted his position. "Joel? Do you see anything?"

"Negative," her brother responded. "If he's smart, he took off upon learning the odds were stacked against him."

Griff grunted but didn't let her up. After another long five minutes, Griff finally stood. "Stay here for a minute. I'll try to draw him out."

"What?" She lifted her head and grabbed his arm to stop him. "You can't use yourself as bait."

"Why not?" He shook off her hand and stepped out from behind the tree. She swallowed hard and watched as Griff slowly made his way to the SUVs.

His was parked beside hers and happened to be closer. He unlocked the car, then ducked inside to check the interior. After a few seconds, Griff gestured to her for the keys. She tugged the fob from her pocket and threw it toward him. He caught it and repeated the process of checking the interior of her vehicle.

When that was finished, he turned. "Joel, I'd like you to ask Royal to track for this guy's scent."

"I'm not sure that's a good idea," Alexis quickly stepped forward. "This guy is armed and has not hesitated to shoot at us. He could take Joel and Royal out in a heartbeat."

"We'll do it," Joel quickly interjected. "I'm with you, Griff. We need to know where he was and if he's still in the area."

"Joel," she protested in exasperation.

Her brother ignored her, turning to his black lab. "Are you ready to search? Huh? Are you?" He offered Royal water. "Search! Search bad guy!"

Despite not having a scent source to work from, Royal turned and lowered his nose to the ground. Alexis shot Griff an annoyed glance, then caught up to her brother. "If you're going, so am I."

She half expected Griff to argue, but he didn't. Maybe he knew it was better for the three of them to stick together.

Joel and Royal led the way. Remembering how Denali had growled seconds before the shock rang out made her wonder if Denali had recognized the scent of the bad guy too. They remained silent, and she knew Griff was keeping a wary eye out for their shooter as Joel focused on his K9.

Royal wound through the trees for a solid fifteen minutes until they came upon what appeared to be a path. It wasn't one that had been used often, but the flattened grass and broken branches from low bushes indicated it had been used recently.

Sure enough, Royal picked up the pace, his tail moving from side to side as he sniffed along the ground. Alexis hoped Denali would alert them if this guy was hiding nearby. As much as she wanted Griff to arrest him, she was half hoping he'd left the area.

Royal veered off the path toward a tree with a low-hanging branch. Then the lab sat and let out a sharp bark.

"This is it." Joel stared up at the tree branch. "He must have climbed up there. There are scuff marks on the bark."

Griff crossed over to see for himself. Joel rewarded his K9, as Alexis glanced around curiously. "I don't see any place where he could have hidden a car."

"Yeah." Griff rubbed the back of his neck. "What about the spent shell casing?"

"Hang on." Joel called Royal over, took the stuffed beaver, and made Royal sit. "Are you ready to search? Search for gold."

Royal jumped to his feet, spun in a circle, and pushed through the brush, his nose close to the ground. She and Denali stayed back, giving Joel room to work.

Within minutes, Royal let out a bark. He didn't sit because the brush was so thick. Joel shoved the branches aside, peering at the ground.

"Found it." Her brother glanced at Griff. "Have another evidence bag?"

"Yes." Griff handed it over. Joel carefully picked up the shell casing, then passed the bag back. Griff examined it, then glanced back up at the branch overhead. "I hope the lab is able to match this with our previous casing."

She nodded. "I'm sure it's the same guy, but having proof would be nice."

"This was definitely his perch." Joel backed out of the brush, taking a moment to pluck the prickers from his clothes. Then he rewarded Royal a second time. "Good boy!"

Denali glanced up at her, as if asking why she was left out of the game. Alexis stroked her fur. "Next time."

Denali wagged her tail as if in agreement.

"Let's head back to the cars." Griff pocketed the second shell casing, then frowned. "I confess, I wasn't paying attention to my compass."

"I was," Joel said. "We'll find our way back, no problem."

"I double-checked our location too." Alexis turned to follow Joel.

"I feel like a dope," Griff muttered, his cheeks red. "I was too focused on watching the trees to make sure he didn't jump out at us."

"You're not a dope, verifying our location is

second nature for those of us using K9s to track scents." She managed a weary smile. "It only takes one time getting lost before you make it a habit."

"I can imagine." Griff shook his head. "I have a lot to learn about what you and your siblings do."

She didn't know how to answer that, so she fell silent. While there was no hurry, she'd noticed Joel set a brisk pace. She didn't mind, and glancing at Griff, she was relieved he wasn't limping.

When they reached the clearing, she moved toward her vehicle. "Hey, Griff? I need the key."

"I'd like you and Denali to ride with me," Griff said. "I don't like how this guy climbed a tree with his rifle to shoot at you."

As much as she didn't like it either, she didn't appreciate being ordered to give up her car. "I'd rather use my own vehicle." She held out her hand, wiggling her fingers. "The key, please."

Joel and Royal came up beside her. "You should go with Griff," Joel said. "Chase would want you to be safe."

"Go where?" It was difficult to maintain her composure. As much as she had already accepted the fact that this guy had set up here to eliminate her, she wasn't about to go along with a plan she didn't understand. "What's the point? We're heading back to the ranch, aren't we?"

"Where we have two pregnant women and a

child?" Joel asked, referring to Maya and Chase's wife, Wyn, and their son, Eli. He shook his head. "I don't think so."

"I suggest we find a place in Greybull to stay for the night." Griff crossed over to her. "Please, Alexis. I need to stay in the area anyway. I promise you'll be safe with me."

She sighed, knowing Joel was right. She would never place her family members in harm's way. Especially not her pregnant sister and sister-in-law and her nephew, Eli. She held Griff's gaze. "Fine. I'll go with you, but you're going to keep me in the loop on this case."

"Of course." Griff nodded and tossed the key fob to her brother. "Thanks, Alexis. Let's hit the road."

Swallowing a sigh, she turned to Joel. "I need supplies for Denali from the SUV."

Her brother opened the back hatch. She stepped forward, rummaging for extra dog food and Denali's bullet-resistant K9 vest. Denali's regular vest was lightweight for the summer months. The Kevlar vest weighed a ton and would not only slow the K9 down, but it would also add to the need for frequent rest breaks.

The inconvenience was nothing, though, compared to protecting Denali. Summer or not, she would insist the dog wear the Kevlar vest out in the field from this point forward.

She double-checked her backpack to make sure she had what she needed, then stepped back. "Come, Denali." She moved toward Griff's SUV. "We'll put her in the back. You don't have a crate barrier, but it will have to do."

"I can buy one," he offered.

"No need." She waved that off. "This is a temporary arrangement."

"Do you want me to follow you into Greybull?" Joel asked. "We can meet for dinner and discuss options."

"Dinner sounds great. I'm starved." Griff swept his gaze around the clearing one last time. "Let's get out of here."

"Jump up!" Alexis gave Denali the hand signal to get into the back of Griff's vehicle. The dog did so, then stretched out and rested her head between her paws. She stroked a hand over Denali's soft fur. "You worked hard today, didn't you? You deserve to rest now."

Denali thumped her tail at the sound of her voice, then closed her eyes.

Alexis stepped back and closed the hatch. Then she shrugged out of the pack and her utility belt, setting both items along with the extra supplies on the floor of the back seat.

When they were finally on the road, she glanced at Griff. "Do you have any leads on this guy? A place to start looking for him?"

"Not exactly." Griff sighed, then asked, "Is it possible you know him?"

She reared back in horror. "No! How could you ask me that?"

"Hear me out," Griff said. "You grew up in this area. Is there anyone you can think of who is capable of this? A guy from your school maybe? Or working in the area? Maybe someone who gave off a bad vibe?"

She sat back in her seat. "Nobody comes to mind, but if we're talking about high school, I need to think about it." She had done tutoring for several younger classmates in English and history. A boy named Kyle had mentioned his dog had died recently, and when she'd expressed condolences, he just shrugged and changed the subject. She hadn't thought much about it. And his blasé attitude certainly didn't make him a serial killer.

She couldn't imagine anyone she knew on a first-name basis was capable of brutally murdering young women, then coming after her. It seemed as if that would take someone evil. Kyle had been appreciative of her help. So had her other students. Not one of them had come across as capable of doing something like this.

Yet there have been some serial killers like Ted

Bundy, who had displayed an outwardly charming and charismatic personality.

She shivered. It was horrible to think that someone she knew on a personal level had done this. But deep down, she knew anything was possible.

GRIFF NAVIGATED the highway back to Greybull. There was more traffic on the roads than usual, but that could be a lingering effect of the Fourth of July holiday. He was glad that was behind them, or it would have been that much more difficult to find a hotel room.

The tourist season in Wyoming was short. In the fall, hunters came out in droves too. Some of them, though, brought their own campers to stay closer to the areas where they planned to hunt.

Knowing there were many strange faces around town would make it difficult to pinpoint his unknown subject. Was he wrong to believe the guy might be a local? He wasn't a profiler like Agent Cheri Artez, but it made more sense to him that the killer had chosen the dump site somewhere closer to his home base.

He kept a wary eye on the rearview mirror but needn't have worried. Joel stayed close behind them.

He couldn't see Denali and imagined she was stretched out and sleeping. He didn't blame the dog for being tired. He was exhausted too. And hungry. The hour was going on five in the evening, and he hadn't eaten anything substantial since breakfast.

He didn't have Joel's number, so when they approached the city limits of Greybull, he turned to Alexis. "Call your brother, have him meet us at Della's Diner."

"Okay." She lifted her phone. "Joel? Griff wants to meet at Della's Diner." She listened for a minute, then sighed loudly. "Why on earth would Jess and Logan tell Chase? You know overprotective he can be." Another pause, then, "Yeah. Okay. See you soon."

"Problems?" Griff asked.

"No." Alexis looked frustrated. "Chase wants me to call. Apparently, he's upset I didn't fill him in personally on everything that went down today. As if I'm not sitting next to the FBI."

Griff shrugged. "He's family. And somewhat of a father figure to the rest of you, right?"

"He's family, and yeah, he and Maya stepped forward to keep us together after our parents died, but sometimes he takes it to an extreme." She tucked the phone away. "I'll call him after we eat and are settled in the hotel."

He would have encouraged her to call now, but

the sign for Della's Diner was up ahead. Despite the early hour, the parking lot was packed. He swallowed a groan, hoping there would be at least one empty table available.

"Please open the hatch for Denali." Alexis pushed out of the passenger seat.

He did so, then shut down the engine. Joel had to settle for a spot farther down because of the limited options.

"Don't worry, girl," Alexis said to her dog. "You can sleep under the table while we eat."

Joel and Royal strode toward them. "Too many tourists," Joel grumbled. "I hope we don't have to wait."

"Me too." Griff headed to the door, holding it open for Alexis.

Thankfully, a table of four stood to leave when they walked in. Alexis slipped past them to snag the booth, stacking the few empty dishes to the center of the table. Griff was a little surprised that Royal and Denali crawled beneath the table to sleep. He'd figured they'd want to play, but the events of the day had worn them out.

It didn't take long for a young, harried server to clear the dishes and wipe the table down. "What can I get you?"

"I'll have the chicken sandwich with fries, thanks," Alexis said.

"Cheeseburger and fries for me," Griff said.

"Add another cheeseburger with fries for me," Joel added. "Thanks."

"Anything other than water to drink?" Griff could see the server's name was Cyndi. She was young enough that he wanted to warn her to be careful. "Iced tea? Soft drinks?"

When she'd gotten orders for a ginger ale for Alexis and iced teas for him and Joel, Cyndi hurried away.

"It's hard not to look at her and see a potential victim," Alexis said in a low voice.

"I had the same concern." Griff scrubbed his hands over his face. "I need to figure out who this guy is and where he's holding these women before he kills them."

"Do you think the profiler will help with that?" Alexis's expression held doubt. "What can she tell from three victims?"

"In theory, the profiler can narrow down the suspect pool, but in this case, I'm not sure that will help." He didn't want to disparage a colleague he hadn't even met. "Most serial killers are usually white males between the ages of twenty and forty who tend to be loners who don't mingle well with society."

"Unless he's that old guy in New Jersey who had a wife, kids, and still killed women," Joel drawled.

"Or Ted Bundy who charmed women into his car," Alexis added.

"I know. There are plenty of serial killers who don't fit the typical profile." Griff shook his head, feeling helpless. "Which makes our job more difficult. And out here in Wyoming, there are more men than women in general, so that makes it even harder to narrow the pool of suspects. Not to mention being a loner out here isn't that unusual. Avoiding the crowded city is a big reason people move here in the first place." The more he thought about how he'd find this guy, the more he feared his efforts would be too little too late.

For Megan and anyone else who may have caught this guy's attention. *Like Alexis*, he thought grimly.

Cyndi returned with their order. The food smelled amazing, making Griff's mouth water. But he knew better than to snitch a fry. He folded his hands and looked at Alexis and Joel. One of them would want to say grace.

The Sullivans always said grace.

"Your turn," Joel teased.

"Okay." She bowed her head. "Dear Lord Jesus, we thank You for this food we are blessed to eat. We ask that You keep Wendy Evers safe in Your loving arms. And please guide Griff and the other police officers as they seek to find her. Amen."

"Amen," Joel echoed. A half second later, Griff added, "Amen."

Was God really listening to Alexis's prayer? He wasn't sure, but at this point, he would take all the help he could get. Wendy didn't deserve whatever she was suffering through.

No woman did.

Taking a large bite of his burger, he tried not to moan with appreciation. He drank half his tea in one long gulp, then reached for his water. He felt dehydrated from being out in the sun most of the day and knew Alexis and Denali had been out there longer.

"I can't think of anyone who could be involved in this," Alexis said, after they ate in silence for a few minutes. "I mean, sure, there were a couple of kids who didn't fit in with the rest of us. But I can't see any of them doing something like this."

"Why do you think Alexis knows the guy?" Joel asked with a frown.

"Not just Alexis, you and even your other siblings," Griff said. "If this guy is native to the area, it's likely one of you has run into him at one time or another."

"Local to Greybull or Cody?" Alexis asked. "The two towns aren't that close. And they have their own high schools. Although, I know some of the kids from outside Greybull preferred coming to

Cody, despite the distance. Cody had better sports teams."

"Both, I guess." Griff munched a french fry. "Maybe you're right and I'm grasping at straws. I don't have much to go on." He abruptly pulled the second shell casing he found from his pocket and pushed it across the table to Joel. "I need a favor. Take this back to the ranch so Logan can drop this off at the lab with the first one. I'm really hoping we get fingerprints off them."

"Sure." Joel nodded, stuffing it into his pocket. "Happy to help."

The shell casings were the best lead he had. Unless there was something more to be learned from the autopsies. He made a mental note to check in with the ME's office first thing tomorrow.

He reached for his wallet, but Joel snatched the bill before he could look at it. "We've got this."

"I can pay," he protested.

"Too late." Joel grinned as he tossed cash onto the table. "Let's go, there's a line forming at the door."

"What's the hotel situation in this town?" Griff asked Alexis once they were back in his SUV.

"I think there's one on the west side of town. Not that I've personally stayed there," she hastily added. "So don't blame me if it's a dump."

He didn't want to take Alexis to a dump, but he

suspected there weren't many options. The town of Greybull was much smaller than Cody. Was his unknown subject here or in Cody? Or somewhere else entirely? For all he knew, the killer could be halfway to Sheridan or some other town by now.

The hotel wasn't as bad as he'd feared, and Griff was able to get a small suite on the ground floor to accommodate Denali. He carried in the extra dog supplies, leaving her to bring her backpack.

"A suite?" Alexis shot him an amused look as she fed Denali. "Expensive."

"Necessary." He could feel the tips of his ears burning with embarrassment. "You and Denali can have the bedroom. I'll make do with the sofa sleeper."

"Okay." She yawned, shrugged out of her backpack, and plopped onto the couch. "I'm too tired to argue with you."

"Good, because that wouldn't change my mind anyway." He stifled a yawn, knowing he was tired enough to sleep anywhere. He set the dog supplies on the table and dropped beside her, rubbing his sore knee.

"Oh, that reminds me." She pulled her pack over and rummaged inside. "I have ibuprofen for you."

"Really?" He gratefully accepted the bottle. "Thanks."

Denali finished eating and came over to stretch out on the floor at their feet. Alexis sighed. "I don't know about you, but I think we'll go to bed early."

"I'm with you on that." He downed the pills, hoping they would kick in fast.

They sat in silence for a few minutes. But then Denali went to the door, looking over her shoulder at Alexis. "Time to go out, huh, girl?"

Griff accompanied the pair outside. There were lots of people milling about, which wasn't helpful as he tried to be on alert for danger. But they weren't out there long. Denali got down to business, and Alexis quickly cleaned up after her. Less than five minutes later, they were back inside.

"Good night, Griff." Alexis gave him a quick smile, then disappeared into the bedroom, closing the door behind her.

He unfolded the sofa bed and took off his shoes and set his gun aside, before stretching out with a low groan. Why did he feel every one of his thirty-seven years? He must have fallen asleep because the next thing he knew, sharp barking woke him.

Denali? Griff rolled off the sofa sleeper and reached for his gun. The last time Denali had growled and barked, the perp had been nearby and tried to shoot Alexis.

Could his suspect be outside now? He lunged

for the door, quickly flipping the locks and heading down the hall. If this guy was out there, he was determined to get him into custody.

5

Denali's barking pulled Alexis from a sound sleep, but her senses immediately went on high alert. She shoved her feet into her shoes and reached for the Glock she'd removed from her backpack and set on the bedside table. She would not hesitate to protect herself and Denali.

Wishing she hadn't left the window open to allow the cool breeze to filter in, she whispered, "Come, Denali." Her K9 trotted to her side. Keeping away from the window as much as possible in the small room, she edged toward the door.

She didn't hear anything from the main room. Was it possible Griff hadn't heard Denali? She opened the door, then quickly darted through the opening. Denali was her shadow at her side.

"Griff?" Sweeping her gaze over the room, her

chest tightened when she realized it was empty. The main door was shut, but the chain lock and deadbolt had been disengaged.

He'd gone out after this guy!

Without thinking it through, she opened the door to follow. Squinting against the glare, she hurried down the hall to the side exit they'd used earlier to take Denali out to get busy.

The door was made of glass, giving her pause. With the bright overhead lights, she couldn't see through the darkness beyond the door. She moved to the left side of the hallway, keeping the weapon down at her side.

Denali was on alert too. When she finally reached the door, she was grateful there was nobody lurking immediately outside the door. Beyond that? She swallowed hard and pushed the door open to step out.

"Stop! FBI!" Griff's curt demand rang through the silence of the night.

Her pulse shot into triple digits. Bringing her weapon up and holding it in both hands, she inched along the side of the building, trying to see where Griff and the killer were located.

Pop! Pop!

No! Griff! Alexis was about to send Denali out to search for the bad guy as a distraction, when she spotted Griff crouching near a tree that appeared to be directly across from their room.

She didn't see anyone else. Where was the shooter?

She hesitated, unwilling to distract Griff by announcing her presence. She couldn't see anyone and wondered if Griff had lost sight of him too.

After a long minute, she finally called, "Griff? Can you see him?"

"No." He sounded disgusted. Then he turned to glance at her. "Can Denali find him?"

"I think so." Swallowing against a lump of fear, she crouched near her dog. "Search! Search bad guy."

If Denali was confused by the new command, her K9 didn't show it. Denali quickly darted toward the grove of trees where Griff was located. She sniffed along the ground and then spent a long moment at the base of a tree barely ten feet from where Griff was.

Her dog sat and looked up at her. Denali didn't bark, maybe because she wasn't searching for napoo.

"Good girl," she praised in a hushed tone. "Search. Search bad guy."

Denali turned and lowered her snout to the ground. Her K9 moved silently through the trees, sniffing with interest. Alexis stayed close, feeling Griff coming up behind her.

"Be careful," he warned.

"We will." She still carried her weapon in both hands. Watching the woods and her dog at the same time made her worry she wouldn't see the threat until it was too late.

Lord Jesus, keep us safe in Your care!

Denali broke through the trees. Alexis realized they were on a dead-end road. There were a lot of those in these small towns, she knew. Only the state highways connected one town to the next.

Catching a glimpse of red taillights rounding a corner, she knew they were too late. In the darkness, she couldn't tell what the make or model of the car was, other than it looked to be an SUV, not uncommon for Wyoming. Driving anything without four-wheel drive was foolish.

Denali trotted a few yards down the road, then stopped to sniff with interest. Then she sat and stared up at Alexis.

"Good girl!" She didn't bother to whisper now that the threat was gone. Running her fingers over Denali's fur, she lavished praise on her dog. "Good girl. You knew just what to do! I'm so proud of you!"

"He shot at me long enough to escape." Griff scowled. "The bigger question is how he knew we were here? Even if he had memorized my SUV license plate, how did he know which room we were staying in?"

"I'm not sure." She stood and tucked her weapon into her waist band. "Maybe he was making his way around the building when Denali caught his scent. I had the window open, and the wind is coming from the east."

"I'm grateful we had your dog to alert us." Griff scowled. "I need a replacement SUV and something more to go on to find this guy."

She understood his frustration. It was concerning that this guy had tracked them down here at all.

"Let's head back." Griff turned to walk back through the trees. She waited a moment for Denali to get busy before they followed. He shook his head. "This is not typical behavior from a serial killer. Only in very rare cases have they turned their attention to the agent trying to find them. Honestly? I'd have expected him to go underground. To lie low until the heat was off and he could continue hunting his next victim."

A chill snaked down her spine. "He's not fixated on you as the federal agent, but on me." Alexis swallowed hard. "I'm his target."

His scowl deepened as he opened the side exit using his key. Good thing he had his, as hers was inside. "I need to get you in protective custody."

"No." She urged Denali to go in first, then followed. "There's no reason to take drastic action. If he really tracked your SUV, then swapping the car should work. Besides, I want to help you find him."

He didn't look happy as he unlocked the door to their room. Then Denali brushed past him, and his expression softened. "I can't believe she tracked him to the road."

"I guess I should have agreed to cross-train her to track humans too." Alexis found the pink piggy and threw it up for Denali. The reward was a little late, but she figured her dog was smart enough to make the connection. "I was in California searching for wildfire victims when Maya had the trainer come back to give tips on cross-training. Since Denali is our only cadaver dog, I didn't think it was a good idea at the time."

"I understand." He stood off to the side to give them room. "You wanted Denali focused on finding your parents."

"Yes. And to work disaster scenes." She scooted around the open sofa sleeper to reach the small kitchenette. It was going on four in the morning now, and she needed coffee. "I had hoped we'd have answers on what happened to our parents by now."

As she made coffee, Griff folded the sofa bed away. Then he moved to the window to peer outside. "It's too early to get a rental car, but we should get out of here."

"Most cafés aren't open for breakfast yet." When the coffee finished brewing, she poured two cups, handing one to Griff. "As far as the rental car, we have a spare SUV at the ranch. I can ask a couple of my siblings to bring it. We won't meet here at the hotel," she added. "We'll find a neutral location."

He considered that for a moment, then nodded. "I feel bad your family is footing the bill for all of this. I'll work with my boss to reimburse your expenses."

"Don't worry about that." She sipped her coffee. "You could always add a second bag of dog food as payment."

As she'd hoped, that made him smile. "At least two bags. I want you to know how much I appreciate you and Denali finding our victims."

"I'm glad we were able to do that." Her expression turned somber. "Who will tell their families?"

"I should be the one to handle the notification," Griff admitted. "Unfortunately, Josie Allen doesn't have family. And Megan only has a brother who lives in Arizona. I don't want to leave the state, so I'll send the local law enforcement officials to make that notification. He can call me with questions."

She nodded, thinking of how she'd camp out at the FBI office building in Cheyenne if anything happened to one of her siblings. "Has he been interviewed?"

"Not by me, yet. The locals spoke to him after the grocery store staff notified the police that Megan hadn't been to work or at home. Her phone has been off since she finished her shift at the store. I need to speak with him, too, but ended up focusing on the most recent missing girl." He shrugged, then added, "Megan's brother Tom wasn't here in town, and according to the police report, he didn't know if she was seeing anyone. I figured that interview could wait until I spoke to Wendy Evers's grandmother."

"That makes sense." She didn't blame him for focusing on Wendy's case. Every hour that passed made it less likely they'd find the young woman in time to save her.

If it wasn't already too late. Considering how the killer had stayed in the area to come after her, she felt certain he'd either tied Wendy up in a cellar somewhere or had already killed her.

Most likely the latter.

Still, she wouldn't give up hope. "Maybe Tom Riley will drive up from Arizona to speak to you in person."

"That's the goal." He scrubbed his face with his hands. "I need to find this guy, and soon."

She empathized with his despair and set her

empty coffee mug aside. "I'm going to take a quick shower. I have a spare shirt in my backpack." She grimaced, then added, "I'll ask my brothers to bring a change of clothes for you too."

"I have an extra shirt in my car, but thanks for the offer." He flashed a lopsided smile. "I'll use the shower when you're finished. By then, we should be able to find a place to have breakfast."

"Okay." She headed to the bedroom. Denali followed and stretched out in front of the door as if to protect her.

It felt good to change into a clean shirt after sleeping in her clothes. While Griff took his turn, she fed Denali. It was early, but she had some of Anna's homemade sweet potato dog biscuits in her pack that she could give Denali later.

"Did you call your family yet?" Griff asked when he emerged from the bedroom. He wore a clean dark-green shirt that emphasized his eyes. He looked so handsome she had to tear her gaze away.

"Ah, not yet." She glanced at her watch; it was twenty minutes past five in the morning. "It's early, although knowing Justin, he's up working with the horses by now."

"We can wait until after we've had breakfast." Griff holstered his weapon. "I was thinking we should walk to the café. Leaving the car here may convince this guy we're still in the room."

"Fine by me." She glanced at Denali. The shooter obviously knew her dog by sight, which could be a problem. "We'll have to be careful. If he's stationed somewhere close by, he might see us."

"I know." Griff had pulled up the map app on his phone. "There aren't as many back roads here as there are in Cheyenne." He stepped close so she could see his screen. "If we go this way, we may be able to get there without being seen."

He was so close that the tantalizing scent of the hotel shampoo teased her senses. She forced herself to nod. "Sounds good."

He smiled. Then his gaze dropped to her mouth. For long seconds, neither of them moved. Was he going to kiss her?

Then the moment passed when he stepped back. "Let's go."

Fighting a flash of disappointment, she shoved the rest of Denali's things into her backpack.

This wasn't the time or place to think about kissing Griff. Not when there was a serial killer on the loose.

GRIFF TRIED to shake off the sizzling awareness shimmering between them. Alexis was too young for him even if he was interested.

Which he wasn't.

Yeah, and maybe if he told himself that, say, a hundred times, he'd start to believe it.

Grace had been gone for two years, and up until a few months ago, he'd thought of her almost every day.

Now Alexis dominated his thoughts.

Not good. He needed to stay focused on finding this killer.

He opened the door and peered into the hallway. Seeing nothing, he stepped back and held the door for Alexis and Denali. She shrugged into her backpack and crossed over to join him. "We'll use the exit on the opposite side of the hallway. Not the one we used earlier."

She nodded in understanding and led the way. Griff followed her and Denali as they headed outside. Even in July, the mornings could be cool, but today seemed to be an exception. A warm breeze washed over them as they took a circuitous route away from the hotel.

He kept a sharp eye out for his suspect, but the hour was early enough that there weren't many people up and around. It wouldn't take long for the tourists to flock to the streets.

"Hold on." He snagged Alexis's arm when an SUV pulled out of a gas station parking lot. The driver's side window was down, and he briefly wondered if Denali would pick up the driver's scent. The white car sped past them without seeming to notice or care that they were there. He relaxed and let her go. "Sorry. I guess I'm a little on edge."

"With good reason." She managed a wan smile. "Let's hope he's far away by now."

Griff had no intention of banking on that. Not when this guy was clearly becoming obsessed with Alexis. He hoped to convince her siblings to take her back to the ranch. He knew she didn't want to place her family in danger, but she would be much safer there with people around, not to mention nine dogs. *Ten*, he silently amended as they turned down a side street to cut through a parking lot. There was the new puppy, Bear, who was growing like crazy.

Alexis would never move, yet another reason he needed to ignore his attraction to her. Despite covering the entire state, he had to live in Cheyenne where the federal office building was located.

"Hey, the Corner Café is open," Alexis said, interrupting his thoughts. "I could sure use more coffee."

He wouldn't mind coffee and food. "Hopefully, they won't mind Denali."

"They won't. We've been here before." She sounded certain, so he didn't argue.

They were on the opposite end of the city from Della's Diner, but the menu was much the same. As the first customers, they had their pick of seats. Alexis chose a booth in the corner. He took the side where he could keep an eye on the door. Alexis sat across from him. Denali crawled under the table and stretched out at her feet.

"Coffee?" A middle-aged woman with brassy-blond hair came over with two mugs and a full pot. Her name tag read Louise.

"Yes, please," he and Alexis said in unison.

Louise laughed, poured their coffee, and tapped the plastic menus. "Let me know when you're ready to order."

Griff took the menu, already knowing he'd have his usual. He noticed Alexis didn't bother to check it out. "You know what you'd like?"

"Yes." She flushed. "I love their veggie omelet. I'll call my family as soon as we order."

Louise returned and refilled their coffee mugs before pulling out her pad. He asked for two eggs over easy with toast, bacon, and hash browns. Alexis ordered the veggie omelet with fruit.

Sipping his coffee, he listened as she made the call.

"Hi, Anna, it's Alexis. Is Joel or Justin around? I'm fine, just need a favor." She waited silently for a moment, then, "Hey, Joel. Everything is fine." She rolled her eyes. "The shooter did show up at the hotel early this morning, so I need you and Justin or whoever is around to bring two SUVs. We'll use one here; you can ride the other one back home."

He could tell by her relieved expression her siblings were going along with the plan.

"Great, thanks. We're at the Corner Café on the west side of town. Thanks, Joel." She lowered the phone. "They'll hit the road ASAP."

"Good." He knew the Sullivan K9 ranch was about forty-five minutes away. He'd never been there but had looked it up online. Their website was nothing fancy. Most of their business came through local law enforcement agencies and word of mouth.

He admired their dedication to serving the community.

When their breakfasts arrived, he glanced at Alexis, knowing she'd want to say grace.

She surprised him by reaching across the table to grasp his hand. Her warm fingers curled around his, making it difficult to think straight.

"Dear Lord Jesus, we thank You for this food we are blessed to eat. We ask for You to continue keeping Wendy Evers safe in Your care. And please guide us to the man who seeks to do harm. Amen."

"Amen." He forced himself to release her hand. "Thanks, Alexis."

"Of course." She reached for her fork.

He dove into his meal. The hash browns were crispy, just the way he liked them. Under the table,

Denali brushed against his legs as she switched positions.

"I've been thinking about what you said, about kids from school who could do something like this." She lifted her blue eyes to his. "There was a kid named Brent Wilson who was arrested for sexual assault." She shrugged. "From what I heard, the charges were dropped to sexual misconduct, and he didn't do much if any time in jail."

That intrigued him. "Brent Wilson? He's from Cody?"

"Yes. I hate to accuse him unfairly but thought you should know."

He glanced at his watch. Still too early to contact the lab in Cheyenne, but if there were fingerprints on the shell casings, this could be the break they needed. "That's great, Alexis. Keep throwing names out there. I won't accuse anyone without proof, so don't let that hold you back."

She sighed. "There are too many names to do that."

"Not if you focus on those kids who were loners, those considered unpopular by teenage standards." His pulse had kicked up with anticipation. "Anything could help, Alexis."

She ate in silence for several minutes, her expression thoughtful. "I don't know. Let me think about it."

They dawdled over breakfast, waiting for her brothers to arrive. A few more customers came in. Thankfully, it was early enough that he didn't feel too guilty over hogging a table.

When Alexis's phone rang, she quickly answered. "Hey, Joel. Really?" She frowned, looking at her watch. "That's fast. What did you do, speed here?" Another pause, then, "Okay, great. See you both soon."

"I can't believe they got here so quickly."

"I know. Joel and Justin have gotten their share of speeding tickets when they were younger. Chase threatened to take their licenses away if they didn't shape up." She smiled. "The state patrol doesn't bother to pull anyone over unless they're doing more than fifteen miles over the posted limit."

He sat back as Louise brought more coffee. "We have two more joining us, and I suspect they'll want to eat too."

"Great." Louise brightened. "Let me know when they're ready."

As if on cue, two men entered the café, a dog on either side of them. Joel and Justin were identical twins, but there were enough differences that he'd learned to tell them apart. Joel was slightly shorter and bulkier around the shoulders. Justin was lean and wore his brown hair short compared to Joel, who wore his long enough to brush against the back of his collar. They shared Alexis's blue eyes.

In addition to Joel's black lab, Royal, Justin was accompanied by a yellow lab named Stone. He'd learned the Sullivan family had chosen a national park theme when it came to picking names for their dogs. When they arrived at the table, he and Alexis scooted over to make room. Without being told, both dogs crawled underneath to join Denali. The animals were clearly familiar with the routine.

"Smells great!" Justin plucked a menu from the rack behind the condiments. "I'm all in on the farmer's omelet."

"I need coffee," Joel muttered. "Breakfast too," he added when Alexis arched a brow. "We were up early. Logan and Jess left at first light to get the evidence to the lab in Cheyenne."

Griff nodded. "Thanks. That means a lot."

"With Joel's help, we got through the morning chores faster than usual," Justin added.

Louise returned with coffee for the twins. Then she took their orders.

"Fill us in on what happened," Joel said when she'd left. "I don't like the idea of this guy finding you at the hotel."

Griff provided a quick rundown on the early morning events. "The only explanation I have is that he recognized my SUV. If not for Denali's barking, we wouldn't have known he was out there."

"He fired twice at Griff, then escaped," Alexis said. "Denali followed his scent to a dead-end road."

"Denali did that?" Joel glanced beneath the table where the dogs were all tangled together. "Good girl."

"I'm concerned this guy has focused his attention on Alexis," Griff said. Joel turned to look at his sister.

"Did you tell Griff about your ex-boyfriends?" Joel frowned as if searching his memory. "Ricky Travers and Oliver Sacks? One of them could be involved."

"No. A lousy cheating boyfriend does not equate to being a serial killer." Alexis scowled. "I don't think this guy is someone that was close to me. A guy from school, maybe. But not a former boyfriend."

Griff tended to agree, although he filed the two names away for later. It wouldn't hurt to run a deep-dive background check on them. Along with Brent Wilson. After Louise brought the twins their breakfast, he asked, "Does anyone else come to mind?"

The twins looked at each other and shrugged. "You can try Brent Wilson," Joel said. "Rumor has it he liked to get handsy with the girls. One slugged him for his efforts."

"I didn't slug him." Alexis scowled. "I shoved him against the locker, kicked him in the groin, and told him if he touched me again, I'd make him pay."

Griff narrowed his gaze. "You left out the part where you were the sexual assault victim."

"Not me," she quickly denied. "Although maybe I should have reported him. He assaulted a girl named Maria Gomez."

"Maria claimed he grabbed her breasts and shoved himself up against her," Justin added. "I don't blame her for filing charges. Not that it did much good."

"It sort of did," Joel argued. "Brent was kicked out of school."

The more he heard about this Brent Wilson, the more he liked him as a suspect. The sooner he got the results from the lab on the shell casings, the better.

6

———————

Alexis wasn't convinced Brent Wilson was the serial killer, but investigating crimes wasn't her area of expertise. Her brothers muttered a quick prayer, then dove into their meals. She was annoyed they'd brought up her old boyfriends.

Lots of guys weren't faithful to their wives or girlfriends. That didn't make them more likely to become a monster who strangled women to death. It made them players who had no interest in settling down, despite their claims to the contrary.

The shell casings they'd found should help narrow their search. In a way, she hoped Brent was the killer, as they'd be able to find and arrest him. Knowing who they were going after was half the battle.

"When does the lab open?" Alexis reached beneath the table to stroke Denali's fur. It was crowded under there with three dogs, but they didn't seem to mind. Playtime could get rambunctious at the ranch, but the K9s knew this wasn't the place for that.

"Seven thirty." Griff looked at his watch. "But the lab techs don't come in until eight."

"Logan and Jess were going to try to be there by eight," Justin said as he ate. "Logan said he knew where it was located."

"This isn't the first time he's taken evidence to the lab," Alexis said. "He helped Doug back in January."

"I remember," Joel said.

"I appreciate Logan's help." Griff sipped his coffee. "As soon as the lab opens, I'll call to have them expedite checking for fingerprints from the casings. Considering we have a missing girl, not to mention two dead bodies, I'm sure they'll accommodate my request."

Alexis was worried about Wendy Evers. She feared the girl might already be dead. That the killer had either buried her someplace else or was hiding her body until he had a chance to get back to the same place that he'd buried the others.

She looked at Griff. "Are you going to keep someone posted at the scene where we found the victims after they're finished looking for evidence?"

He grimaced. "I'd like to, but we don't have the manpower for that."

"What if the killer goes back in a few days to bury Wendy Evers?" She bit her lower lip, and added, "Assuming he's already strangled her."

"I know. I've thought of that." Griff stared down into his coffee mug. "I could rig up a trail cam. See if we can capture him that way."

"That's a great idea." Joel's gaze was full of admiration. "They work pretty well for capturing photos of wildlife."

"Just make sure you put it somewhere this guy won't see it," Justin said. "If he finds it, he'll just pull it down, swipe the SIM card, and do his thing."

"That alone will let us know to head up to find the body," Griff said grimly. "Although I'd rather get a clear picture of him. With our facial recognition software, we'll be able to match him with driver's license photos."

Alexis nodded. "I say we do that first thing. Hopefully, this guy isn't smart enough to anticipate we'd plant a camera."

"Heading up to place the camera works for me." Griff glanced at his watch again. She sensed he was feeling impatient to get to work, but there wasn't much they could do at the early hour. Even during the summer tourist months, stores didn't open until nine in the morning, and it was only seven forty-five now. She could see Griff doing the time calculation in his head. After a long moment, he looked up and held her gaze. "I'd really like you and Denali to head back to the ranch. I can mount the camera and take care of things from here."

"I'm not bringing danger to the ranch." When he opened his mouth to argue, she held up a hand. "This is not negotiable. Besides, this guy is preoccupied with me, which means he's not out there hunting, kidnapping, and harming another girl. If it's too late for Wendy, the least we can do is protect other women."

Griff shook his head. "I refuse to use you as bait."

"Chase would not like that," Joel agreed with a dark frown.

She wasn't fond of that idea herself but forced a smile. "Let's use the word distraction. My presence will keep him distracted and nearby while we gather evidence to identify him."

Griff, Joel, and Justin exchanged pained glances.

"You know I'm right," she added after a long moment. "About being a distraction and keeping the danger away from the ranch."

"You can be the one to tell Chase," Justin said. "He's likely to bite our heads off."

She rolled her eyes. "You make him sound like an ogre. He'll be fine. You can point out that he didn't bring the rest of the family into his predicament back in February for the same reason."

Joel and Justin looked at each other and shrugged. They didn't say anything more as they finished their meals. Louise cleared their plates and left the check on the end of the table. Griff snatched it up before anyone else could move. When he reached into his pocket for his wallet, Justin put a hand on his arm. "We've got this."

"No, I do." Griff frowned. "Your family is doing more than enough to help me. Buying breakfast is the least I can do."

Justin glanced questioningly at her. She shrugged. "I'm sure Griff can put it on his expense account."

Griff nodded, but the way he avoided her gaze indicated he had no intention of doing that. The thought of his expense account reminded her of the FBI profiler that was due to fly into town.

"When does your colleague arrive?" she asked.

"Not sure. I told her to call me when she lands." Griff placed cash on the table. "I need to call the lab, but we'll need someplace safe to hang out before we can buy the trail camera."

"Maybe with the tourists around, we can hide in plain sight." She gestured to the window where the city was beginning to wake up. Even in a town as small as Greybull, there were pedestrians milling about outside, enjoying the warm summer weather. "We can always take Denali to the park."

Griff frowned. "This guy knows what Denali looks like."

That was true, but she couldn't come up with an alternative. "I'm open to other suggestions."

"Try the Greybull campground," Joel suggested. "Plenty of people and your guy probably won't look for you there."

"Okay. That works." Griff looked relieved to have a plan. "Let's get out of here."

Her brother's stood, and their respective K9s quickly scrambled out from beneath the table. Denali emerged last, her tail wagging with excitement at the prospect of playing outside.

She followed her siblings out. Within seconds, the dogs were jumping and running around the open area to the left of the café. She shook her head wryly, then held out her hand. "I need the keys to the SUV."

Joel handed them over. "Are you sure, sis?" He kept his tone low so Griff couldn't hear. "We can find a place in Cody to keep you safe."

"I'm sure." She was touched by his concern. "Thanks, though."

He held her gaze for a long moment. "You care about him, don't you?"

"What?" Her cheeks heated. "No, I mean, yes. Of course, I care about Griff like any other friend. But that's not the reason. I really want him to find this guy. Denali knows his scent and might be able to help us if we get close."

"Royal knows his scent too," Joel said. "I can stick around to work with Griff."

She hated to admit that was true. "I'm the distraction, remember? Just keep your phone close in case we need more K9 support."

"Okay." Joel's expression was resigned. "Justin and I are here if you need us."

"Thanks." She gave him a quick hug. "Be safe driving home."

He nodded and glanced to the trio of dogs. "They act like little kids sometimes."

"Most of the time," she agreed with a laugh. "Until they're asked to work, which for them is just another form of play."

"Here, Stone!" At the sound of Justin's voice, his yellow lab spun and trotted toward him.

"Royal, come!" Joel said. At his command, Royal also returned. Without having anyone to play with, Denali loped to her side.

"By the way, we restocked the SUV." Joel gestured toward the closer of the two SUVs. "There's more dog food, baggies, bowls, and other supplies inside."

"Thanks." She'd anticipated they'd make sure of that. They'd all learned early on to make sure their K9s were well cared for. The safety of their dogs was foremost in their minds. "Don't forget to keep your phones close."

"Ah, Joel? Anna just called." Justin showed him the phone. "There's a lost hiker near Antelope Butte. Apparently, she's been missing since yesterday. Anna wants us to head over right away."

Joel glanced at her. She gave him a shove. "Go. We'll be fine."

Griff came up to stand beside her as the twins and their dogs got settled inside the SUV. Within seconds, they were driving away.

"Does that happen often?" Griff asked, watching them leave.

"Calls for missing hikers? Oh yeah, especially in the summer." She shook her head. "Compass training should be a requirement for anyone who intends to hike in the mountains. It's easy to get turned around."

"I had no idea the calls were that frequent." Griff gestured to the SUV. "Let's head to the campground. It's almost eight. I'll call the lab supervisor from there."

Using the key fob, she opened the back hatch for

Denali. She double-checked the supplies, then stepped back so Denali could jump in. She almost wished now that she hadn't fed Denali early, but Anna's homemade cookie bone would work as a snack later.

She drove through Greybull, heading east toward the campground. She gestured to the right when they passed a hardware store. "That's where we'll find trail cameras."

"Good."

They were asked to pay a fee for a day pass inside the campground. Griff passed the cash over, and they were waved through.

"I like that we had to pay," Griff said. "Makes it less likely my suspect will show up."

"I agree." She pulled over into one of the first empty campsites she found. There was a fire pit and a picnic table. They climbed out and headed to the picnic table. "This is nice."

Griff nodded and reached for his phone. She listened to his side of the call.

"Sue? I'm calling about some evidence that should be arriving at any moment." He paused, smiled, and said, "Great. Yes, Logan is amazing. Listen, I really need those shell casings dusted for prints first thing. This is our only lead to a man who has brutally murdered two young women and likely has kidnapped a third victim." After another pause, he said, "Thank you. I owe you a favor. Call me as soon as you have something."

"That's great that Logan got the evidence there so fast." She bent to stroke Denali who had stretched out at the ground at her feet.

"Yeah, Sue was impressed." He flashed a grin. "Claimed she'd have liked to marry Logan herself if your sister hadn't snatched him first."

"Oh yeah?" She arched a brow. "I'm sure Jess didn't like hearing that."

"Sue Schuman is fifty-three, so I'm sure Jess didn't mind." Griff sat beside her. "So now we sit here and wait for the hardware store to open."

"Yep." She felt bad, but she didn't have a magic wand to make that happen sooner. She dug out her phone. "Let's see if we can find Brent Wilson on social media."

He nodded. "While you do that, I'll get his address from his DMV records."

She listened as he called the office to request the information. She had to go through several Brent Wilsons to find the one who appeared to be roughly the same age as the guy she'd gone to high school with. Unfortunately, his profile picture was him fishing, and there were no recent posts. Nothing for almost two years, she realized with a frown.

Had Brent stopped posting because he'd wanted

to stay off-grid so he could hunt, kidnap, and strangle young women?

"Thanks." Griff ended his call. "The last known address for Brent is Cody, but he's due to have his license renewed next year." He shrugged. "He could have moved without bothering to update his driver's license. A lot of people don't make that a priority."

"Especially not if you're breaking the law." Suddenly she was leaning toward Brent Wilson being their guy. "I guess we'll find out once you get news on the fingerprints."

"Yeah." Griff glanced at his phone. "Here's a picture of his DL. Does he look the way you remember?"

She peered at Brent's face. Truthfully, the photo did not do him justice. It looked like a mug shot, yet she recognized him as the same kid she remembered. "Yes." She handed the phone back. "That's him."

Five minutes later, his phone rang. He quickly answered. "Sue? I hope you have good news for me." As he listened, his face fell. "You're absolutely sure? Yeah, okay. Thanks."

"No prints?"

"Oh, they got a couple of prints, but there's nothing in the system." He sighed. "And they're not a match to Brent Wilson. His fingerprints are on file."

Her stomach knotted. "So we're back to square one."

"Yeah." Griff shook his head. "I should have known it wouldn't be this easy."

Alexis tried to keep a positive attitude. Yet as she gazed out toward the town of Greybull, it was disturbing to realize the killer was still out there.

Ready to strike again.

GRIFF SWALLOWED HIS KEEN DISAPPOINTMENT. The good news was that Sue's tech had lifted several prints. Once they had another suspect, the evidence would help prove his case.

But they still had no idea who this guy was. Or where he was staying.

It was tempting to call back to ask for information on Alexis's former boyfriends, but he refrained. Not liking two men because they'd cheated on a woman he admired and cared about wasn't probable cause.

And he needed to stay focused on who could do something this heinous.

"I'm going to take Denali for a short walk." Alexis jumped up from the bench seat of the picnic table. "She hasn't had much exercise yet today."

"Sounds good." Griff's knee had been stiff that

morning but was already feeling better. The ibuprofen she'd given him had helped. He made a note to ask for more prior to their trek back to the burial site.

Watching Alexis with Denali made him smile. At first, they strolled across the grassy area, but then Alexis returned to get the pink piggy from her backpack.

Intrigued, he watched as she told the dog to sit. Then she walked into the woods. It didn't take long for Alexis to be hidden from view.

"Search!" Alexis called.

Without hesitation, Denali ran straight into the woods, finding Alexis within a matter of seconds. Alexis laughed and threw the piggy back toward the campground. Denali whirled and ran back to get it.

"That's not much of a challenge," he said. "She clearly watched you go into the woods."

"I know. But we'll try again. You're going to help me this time." After she played with Denali for a few minutes, she held out her hand. "Drop."

Denali obeyed, then backed off, as if anticipating another throw. Instead, Alexis crossed over to him. She made Denali turn around so that the K9's back was to the wooded area. "Stay."

Griff was amazed that Denali stayed in place without turning her head. This was an exercise they'd done before. After a long few minutes, Alexis called, "Search!"

Denali wheeled around, lifted her nose to the air, then to the ground. She flawlessly followed Alexis's scent trail until she found her in the woods.

"Good girl." Alexis threw the piggy again.

As much as he enjoyed watching the pair, Griff was anxious to get to work. He needed to follow up with the ME's office regarding the autopsies of Josie Allen and Megan Riley. The killer had used a ligature, so he didn't know if they'd find fingerprints embedded in their skin. Still, the techs could find and isolate hair fibers, skin cells, and other sources of DNA.

Especially if either victim was sexually assaulted.

Too bad Brent Wilson wasn't their guy.

In the middle of their playtime, Denali abruptly turned and stared toward the woods. It was so jarring he found himself searching for what had caught the dog's attention.

"What is it, girl?" Alexis knelt on the grass beside her dog. "What's wrong?"

Denali didn't growl or bark the way she had earlier that morning upon catching a whiff of their bad guy. But her ears were pricked forward, and her gaze seemed to be focused intensely on something he couldn't see.

Griff crossed over to join them. "What caught her attention?"

"I have no idea." Alexis frowned as she straightened. "But I think we'd better find out."

"Okay." He rested his hand on the butt of his weapon. "Stay close in case this guy is hiding nearby."

Alexis nodded. "The wind is coming from the west, so it could be that Denali hasn't scented him yet." She turned to look at him. "Or she could be alerting us to a wild animal threat, like an elk, moose, or some other animal."

He understood. There were plenty of potential threats in the wilderness, and they weren't all walking on two legs. He pulled his weapon from its holster and held it down at his side. "Let's check it out."

Alexis scowled. "You can't go around shooting wildlife with a handgun."

"Only if they attack and our lives are in danger," he agreed. "Trust me, I'd rather not shoot anything."

After a brief hesitation, Alexis nodded and threw her arm toward the woods. "Go, Denali. Search."

Denali glanced up at her as if to make sure, then trotted forward, her nose close to the ground. When they reached the edge of the brush, Denali seemed to quicken her pace. Clearly, she was focused on something.

He just wished he could see what it was. In the distance, he could hear the rumble of voices from other campers, so it didn't seem likely that a bear or some other large animal would be lurking nearby.

Denali pressed forward. Only when they were in the middle of the thicket did the K9 slow down and turn away from the area where the voices were coming from.

"What is it?" Alexis asked again. "What did you find?"

Denali stuck her nose beneath a bush, then began to growl. Griff stopped, lifted his weapon, and swept the area. He didn't see anyone, but could his killer be hiding nearby?

Denali backed away from the bush, her hackles rising as her growls grew louder.

"What is it, girl? Did you find a snake under there?" Alexis appeared puzzled by her K9's behavior.

Denali sat and barked. Holding his weapon up, he stepped in front of Alexis. "Get down. That's her alert, isn't it?"

"Yes." Alexis dropped down to place a protective arm around Denali. "I don't understand. How did this guy get here? And why didn't we see him?"

"I don't know." Griff trusted the dog's keen sense

of smell and hearing more than he trusted his eyesight. But if Denali was alarmed, he was too. He tipped his head to look upward, searching the trees. He knew the guy had climbed a tree back near their SUVs. Maybe he liked being high in a perch, looking down at those he wanted to kill. "We need to back away from here." He kept his tone low. "You and Denali go first. I'll cover you."

"Hold on, I'd like to know what's under that bush." Alexis looked up at him. "If there's not a snake living there, maybe our killer left something behind."

Every instinct in Griff's body told him they needed to get far away from the campground. It had been a bad idea to leave the restaurant. He should have suggested they sit in the SUV at the hardware store to wait for it to open.

Was he overreacting? It didn't make sense that the perp had found them there. He hadn't noticed anyone following them. And if his suspect was hiding and watching them, he likely would have taken a shot by now. He'd done that several times before, including the first time Alexis and Denali had gotten close to his burial ground.

Would Denali alert on a snake? He had no idea. He didn't lower his weapon but nodded toward the bush. "Okay, but be careful. It could be a trap. And stay low, don't make yourself an easy target."

"Understood." Alexis eased up just enough to make her way to the bush. She moved to the side and cautiously shoved the branches out of the way with her arm. Then she frowned. "I don't believe it."

"What?" He couldn't imagine what was under there.

Alexis turned; a grim expression etched on her features. "Do you have another evidence bag?"

"Yes, but tell me what you found." He lowered the weapon and took a few steps toward her. "What did he leave behind?"

"Dog food." Her answer was so unexpected he thought he'd misunderstood.

"Dog food? Why would he bother to do something like that?" Griff lowered the muzzle of his weapon toward the ground as he peered over her shoulder to see what she meant. There was a small pile of dog food beneath the bush.

"I need an evidence bag," Alexis said impatiently. "And we have to call my brothers to have them turn around to come back. I want this dog food tested in a lab ASAP."

"Tested for what?" He pulled a clean evidence bag from the small pouch on his belt and passed it to her. He still didn't understand. "Do you want to know if it's the same brand you use back at the ranch?"

"No, it's not the same brand, the kibble looks

different. The brand of dog food doesn't matter." She used the bag as a glove and put a fistful of the dog food into the bag. Then she stood, eyeing him somberly. "I want this tested for poison."

"Poison?" He glanced over to where Denali sat, watching them with her brown eyes. "How do you know some camper with a dog didn't leave this here? Or dump it because they didn't want to haul it home?"

"I don't think that's what happened." Alexis examined the food inside the evidence bag. "I see what appears to be some moisture on the food. Not enough to make it soggy, but enough to indicate it wasn't sitting under there for a long time."

"Poison," he repeated. "You think the killer purposefully hid dog food hoping Denali would eat it."

"Yes, that's exactly what I think he did." She crossed over to pet her dog. "And this is why we teach our dogs not to eat anything that we don't give them. He must not have realized how well trained our dogs are and how he tipped his hand."

Griff shook his head as the close call sank deep. Not only had this guy somehow figured out where they were, he went a step further to try to kill Denali.

No doubt to get the dog out of the way so he'd have an easier time going after Alexis.

Griff was convinced this serial killer wanted Alexis as his next victim.

7

Simmering anger boiled in Alexis's blood. That this guy would try to poison Denali burned hot. She wanted Griff to find and arrest this killer and soon.

"We need to get out of here." Griff's expression was grim.

She nodded and hurried over to open the back crate area for Denali. She gave her K9 the hand signal to get up, and the collie gracefully leaped inside the SUV. After closing the hatch, she set the evidence bag of poisoned dog food on the floor of the back seat. Seconds later, they were heading out of the park. Instead of turning toward the hardware store, Griff headed in the opposite direction.

"Where are you going?"

"I need to make sure he's not following us." He

glanced at her. "I know a back road that will take us into Greybull. I intend to avoid the main street if possible."

That made sense. Fighting to maintain control, she pulled out her phone. Thankfully, Joel answered on the first ring. "Hey, Alex, what's up?"

"I need you and Justin to come back to Greybull for a few minutes. I know you're supposed to find a missing hiker, but I have a bag of what I believe is poisoned dog food that was set out to entice Denali." Her voice quivered, and she tried to steady herself. They were safe, at least for the moment. "Denali is fine, but we need to get out of here. And I want this food tested in the FBI lab."

"We're turning around now," Joel said. "I can't believe a serial killer would try to harm your dog. It's a personal attack against you."

She silently agreed and knew the attention she'd drawn from this guy was not good. The only reason to harm her dog was so he had a clear path to get to her. She didn't voice her concern, though. No point in getting her brothers riled up. "Thanks, Joel. Call when you're close." Through the side mirror, she could see the town of Greybull disappearing behind them. Griff had headed west rather than east as she'd expected. "We'll find a place to meet."

"Sounds good. Stay strong, sis." Joel had sensed she was on the edge. Justin and Joel were twins, and they were close. But she had a special bond with Joel too. Much the way Trevor had bonded with Kendra.

"I will." She ended the call and stared down at her trembling fingers. Denali wasn't hurt. Her smart K9 had identified the threat. Yet if Denali wasn't so well trained . . .

"Alexis? Are you okay?" Griff's concerned voice broke into her thoughts.

"Yes." She wasn't, but she needed to get over it. God had been watching over them since Denali had found that hand poking out of the earth. She needed to have faith that they would get through this. She drew a deep breath to calm herself. "Joel and Justin are turning around. Hopefully, this won't take too long, and they can get back to Antelope Butte. We'll need to find a place to meet up with them."

"Okay." He passed the next intersection. A mile later, he executed a three-point turn. Twisting in her seat, she peered out the back window. Denali was stretched out in the crate area, likely asleep as if she hadn't narrowly been killed.

"How will we know if we're being followed? We have no idea what vehicle he's driving." Traffic was never a problem in Wyoming, but in summer, there were far more cars on the road than normal. A wave of despair threatened to overwhelm her.

How on earth would Griff find him amid the tourists?

"I know, that's why I did that quick turn." He punched the gas, and the SUV surged forward. His gaze went from the rearview mirror to the highway stretching before them. "So far, so good. Nobody has turned around to follow."

"Okay." She opened and closed her fingers to relax. "I trust you, Griff."

He shot her a quick glance. Then he surprised her by reaching for her hand. "I'll protect you with my life."

Tears welled in her eyes. She blinked them away, hoping he didn't notice. She told herself this was nothing personal. Griff was a federal agent. Of course, he would protect her and any other victim of a crime. He would do the same for Wendy Evers too.

If the young woman was still alive.

Still, his intense green gaze made her think he really meant it. She managed a smile and squeezed his hand. "Thanks. I appreciate your determination to get this guy. I just wish we had more to go on."

"We will. I have a feeling your brother's trail camera idea will help." Griff continued to hold her hand. The warmth of his fingers cradled hers. She admired him and the work he did. Too bad he lived in Cheyenne.

Not that it mattered, she hastily reminded herself. She wasn't interested in pursuing a relationship with Griff or anyone else. And even if she was, attempting another long-distance relationship was not an option.

"I don't think I've been on this road," she said after a few minutes. "This goes into Greybull?"

"Yeah. I got a little lost when I went to see Barbara Evers, Wendy's grandmother, and ended up here." He flashed a crooked smile. "So many of these highways look the same. Since I cover the entire state, it's hard for me to keep track of which one is which."

"For us too," she admitted. "Although since our ranch isn't that far from here, we know Greybull and Cody pretty well."

Soon, the town came into view. Her phone rang. Seeing Joel's name, she quickly answered. "Hey, are you close?"

"Yeah, we're in Greybull now. Where are you?"

"Hang on a minute." She looked for a familiar landmark. "We're on Industrial Avenue coming up on the Attwell Restaurant. Can you meet us in the parking lot?"

"Yep. See you soon."

"I don't think we're too far from the hardware store," Griff said, and he approached the restaurant. "I may head over on foot to avoid attracting attention."

"Maybe you should take one of the twins with you." Oddly, she didn't like the idea of being separated from Griff. "Just in case."

"I can handle it." His offhand comment sparked her anger.

"No, I mean it, Griff." She tightened her grip on his hand. "Please don't go alone. I need you."

He glanced at her in surprise, then slowly nodded. "Okay. Justin can tag along if he's willing. I just hate to make them late for their search."

"It'll be fine." She would make sure Justin accompanied him. This wasn't the time for either of them to go off alone. Especially while the killer was still in the area.

Likely driving around looking for them.

Joel and Justin were waiting in the farthest corner of the parking lot. Griff pulled in beside them and killed the engine. She slid out and opened the back for Denali. Then she reached into the vehicle to retrieve the poisoned dog food. "Here, take it." She thrust the bag toward Joel. "This needs to get to the Cheyenne lab as soon as you're finished searching for your missing hiker. I would be shocked if it wasn't laced with rat poison or some other toxic substance that is harmful to dogs."

"We need to get that guy," Justin muttered.

"I agree." Joel tucked the evidence bag into the SUV. "Don't worry. Once we finish up out here, we'll get Logan to make another trip to Cheyenne." Joel offered a wry grin. "He won't mind. That man is happiest when he's with Jess or flying his plane."

"Thanks." She knew her brother was right. After they were married, Logan and Jess moved into Jess's ranch cabin. Logan had insisted on selling his house in Greybull, and they had built a large hangar near the ranch landing strip to house his three planes. And his tools, of which there were many. Logan either flew planes or worked on them.

Alexis turned to her brother. "Justin, I need you to go with Griff to the hardware store. We didn't get the trail cams yet."

Justin frowned. "Okay, but why the concern?"

"We don't know how the killer found us at the campground." She held her brother's gaze, imploring him to go along with the plan. "What if he's out there, cruising up and down Main Street? I would feel better if he was walking with you."

Justin exchanged a look with Joel, then shrugged. "Sure, why not? I don't mind."

"Thanks." She knew her family would come through for her. "Joel and I will wait here with the dogs. Taking Stone with you will only draw more attention."

"Let's go," Griff said. "The sooner we get those cameras and get out of Greybull, the better."

Alexis watched them go. Feeling Joel's gaze on

her, she arched a brow. "What? This guy is a brutal killer. I doubt he'd hesitate to kill a federal agent."

"You care about Griff," Joel said.

She decided there was no point in arguing. "Yes, I do. That's not the real issue here, though. We need to figure out who this guy is and stop him before he hurts anyone else."

Joel nodded thoughtfully. "Yeah. I'm worried this killer has set his sights on you, Alexis."

She attempted a casual shrug, despite the sick feeling in her stomach. Never in her life had she been targeted by a ruthless killer. She'd never worked in law enforcement the way Maya had. Even Jess used to work the airport with Teddy, who could find drugs. "Maybe. Thanks to Denali, he hasn't gotten too close."

"You need to stay with Griff from here on," Joel said.

Since that was her intent, she simply nodded. "Hey, if you don't mind, I'm going inside to use the bathroom. Keep an eye on Denali for me."

The three dogs were romping in the open field nearby. She didn't think they were visible from the road as they were stationed right behind the restaurant. As she headed inside, she hoped Griff and Justin wouldn't take too long.

When she was finished in the bathroom, she opened the door and almost walked right into a woman waiting. "Oh, sorry," Alexis hastily apologized.

"No problem." The woman tipped her head to the side. "You're Alexis Sullivan, right? You tutored my son in history a few years ago. Kenny? Kenny Tripp?"

"Oh, of course! Nice to see you again, Mrs. Tripp." Kenny was one of five students she'd tutored during her senior year. Kyle, Kenny, David, Tyler, and Steve. "How's Kenny doing?"

"He's great!" Mrs. Tripp's eyes brightened with pride. "He's in his second year of college at Wyoming State."

"I'm so happy for him." Alexis was glad to know her tutoring Kenny had helped. "Tell him I said hi."

"I will. Take care." Mrs. Tripp scooted around her to duck inside the lady's room.

Alexis hurried back outside. Kenny had been a decent kid. Really, they all had. Steve had been the quietest of the group, more withdrawn than the others. Tyler had struggled the most, despite her help, and after a few months of tutoring, he'd stopped coming. Last she'd heard, he'd dropped out of high school. Kyle and David had done okay, though.

Shaking off thoughts of the past, which seemed like another lifetime, Alexis hovered at the main entrance. After watching the street from the doorway for a moment, she headed out. She wanted to run but forced herself to walk calmly around the corner of the building to where the parking lot was located.

As she joined Joel, she glanced at her watch again. Griff and Justin had been gone for twelve minutes.

She lifted her gaze to the sunny sky and silently asked God to keep them safe.

"I RECOMMEND THIS ONE." Justin thrust the box at Griff. "Do you want two just in case?"

"Sure." Griff waited for Justin to grab a second camera.

"Buy a hammer and some nails too," Justin suggested. "I have plenty of gear but no tools in the car."

Griff picked those items up, too, then he turned toward the cash register. He hadn't been separated from Alexis since she'd found the bodies and was struck by how much it had bothered him to leave her behind.

He used the self-checkout register and used his personal credit card rather than his government-issued credit card. His boss haggled over every charge ad nauseam to the point he found it easier to submit a receipt for reimbursement. Granted, that process tended to take longer, but he didn't care.

Outside, he led the way to the back sides of the building to avoid being seen by the people and cars moving up and down the main street. The trip back to the Attwell Restaurant didn't take too long, and when he saw Joel and Alexis standing outside the SUV, a wave of relief washed over him.

"You're back." Her blue eyes lit up when she saw him.

Griff longed to pull her into his arms but managed to hold back. The last thing he wanted was for her brothers to think he might take advantage of her. He smiled and nodded. "I have two cameras. Justin described how they work; it's good they have batteries rather than needing to be charged up. We're set."

"Great." Alexis turned to her brothers. "Let me know when the evidence has been dropped off."

"That's my line," Griff said mildly. Alexis blushed but didn't argue. "I would like to know as soon as the lab has tested the dog food. Make sure you let them know it's related to this serial killer case."

"Okay." Justin opened the back hatch for the labs, taking a moment to give them water.

Joel hesitated. "Are you sure you don't want me and Royal to come with you?"

"I'm sure." Griff wouldn't mind back up, but three people and two dogs would be more noticeable. "Thanks, though. You're helping by getting the evidence to the lab."

"I think we'll head down Main Street," Justin drawled. "Maybe this guy will follow us instead of you."

"Works for me," Joel said.

Alexis frowned. "I don't think that's a good idea. You need to take the back roads the way we are."

Griff kept silent, even though part of him liked the idea of a diversion. Not that he wanted to put any of the Sullivans in danger. Either way, he figured the twins would do what they wanted. Every Sullivan he'd interacted with over the past few years had a stubborn streak. He doubted Justin and Joel were any different.

Joel turned toward Alexis, then gave her a brotherly hug. "Be careful, sis."

"I will." Alexis hugged him back. "You too. I hope you find that hiker. Come, Denali."

As always, Griff was impressed at how well trained the Sullivan K9s were. Denali trotted to Alexis's side. She offered Denali water as well, and the dog lapped eagerly. When Denali finished, Alexis took a moment to hug her dog, stroking her fur before stepping back.

"Get in," she said.

Denali leaped into the back. As soon as they were settled, Griff drove out using the same back road he'd used earlier.

Alexis turned in her seat to watch the rear window for a moment, before settling back. "I'm glad they're not behind us." She glanced at him. "I really don't want my brothers in danger."

"I know." He gestured to the cameras on the floor at her feet. "Once we get them mounted, we'll find a different town to stay in for a while."

She frowned. "Maybe we should head back to Greybull. We know he's been there several times. He may have grown up here or worked here. He seems to know the area well."

"I've considered that," Griff admitted. "But I don't want him to make another attempt to harm you or Denali."

"I get that, but we can't find him if we stay away," she argued.

She was right, but he didn't care. "We'll take things one step at a time. First the cameras. Then we could head to Shell for lunch."

"Lunch?" She shot him an exasperated look. "We just had breakfast."

He shrugged. This little side project would take time. By the time they hiked to the crime scene, mounted the cameras, and headed back out, he would be hungry again.

Under different circumstances, he wouldn't mind hiking the Bighorn Mountains with Alexis.

They rode for several miles in silence. When he finally approached the turnoff where they'd parked last time, he gestured. "Should we park here or try a new spot?"

"New location," Alexis said without hesitation. "Maybe the campground parking lot would be better. More cars there to hide our vehicle. And we can take the same route your suspect used." She grimaced. "Although let's just hope he didn't beat us here."

Griff felt certain the guy was still back in Greybull, but in truth, there had been enough time for the killer to return to this location.

Yet why would he? There's nothing for him here. Just the opposite. Knowing that there may be crime scene techs returning to the burial site should keep him away.

Five minutes later, Griff parked in the campground parking lot, backing the SUV into a space between a large diesel truck and a minivan. Alexis let Denali out of the back, then reached for her backpack.

"I can carry that for you," he offered.

"It's mostly stuff for Denali." She nodded toward the cameras, hammer, and nails. "I'll make room for that."

"Only if you let me carry it," he said. "That hammer and the cameras add weight you shouldn't have to bear."

She reluctantly nodded. "Okay, fine." She knelt on the ground, opened the pack, and moved stuff around. He handed her the cameras, minus the boxes, along with the hammer and nails.

He took the pack and settled it on his shoulders. It was heavier than he'd anticipated.

Alexis gave Denali water, then crossed over to join him. She didn't tell Denali to search, but the K9 had her nose to the ground regardless and trotted toward a familiar group of trees.

"She knows the way, huh?" he asked as they followed the dog.

"Yes." She smiled. "Denali is amazing."

"No argument here." He subtly shifted the pack into a more comfortable position. He was amazed that the Sullivan family carried so much gear for their K9 search and rescue missions. Alexis had carried this pack as if it weighed a feather.

The path Denali took didn't look familiar to him. He pulled out his compass and verified they were headed in the right direction. Not that he didn't trust Denali's nose. Or Alexis's skill. Alexis strode through the woods as if she knew exactly where they were going.

And maybe she did. The Sullivans had combed

the mountainside searching for their parents and pieces of the plane they were in when they'd crashed.

"Do you have any idea what happened to your parents?" he asked.

"No." Alexis's expression turned somber. "They were heading home from a weekend away in Billings. We've considered foul play, but what would have been the motive?"

She had a point. As far as he knew, the Sullivan kids had inherited the ranch through a trust. "I don't know. I guess the crash could have been weather related."

"It was fall and not storming." She glanced at him and shrugged. "Kendra, the youngest believes they were targeted on purpose. But even if that's the case, it's going on six years since they were killed. I highly doubt finding the remains will provide any answers." She looked up at the sky overhead. "I hate to say it, but I think their deaths will remain a mystery."

He nodded in agreement. He knew some cold cases were solved years after the crime had been committed, but those instances were few and far between. Advances in DNA had helped solve some of them, but that was because of the ability to use new technology.

"I've made peace with God over taking our parents," Alexis said. "It helps to know they're in heaven together."

"Losing my wife two years ago was difficult." He surprised himself by mentioning it. "And she was a believer, like you. But I can't get over the fact that God took her from me. There's no reason I should be here, while Grace is gone."

Alexis lightly grasped his arm. "You'll always miss your wife, Griff, the same way we'll always miss our parents. But the truth is they're in a better place. And if you accept Jesus into your heart and soul, you'll see her again one day."

He covered her hand with his for a moment, then stepped away. "I don't know, Alexis. Maybe you're right." He paused near the cluster of trees where the K9s had alerted on the shell casing. There was a clear view from this hilltop to the burial site below. "There certainly is enough evil in the world."

"Exactly, and Jesus is the light of hope." She followed his gaze. "We should give Denali a break before we head down there."

He shrugged out of the pack so she could access the water and collapsible dog bowl. Then she dug out what appeared to be a rectangle-shaped cookie. She offered it to Denali who eagerly chomped on it.

"Sweet potato dog treat," Alexis explained. "Anna makes them."

He stared down at the area below. Was it his imagination, or was there an area beyond the two gravesites that had been disturbed recently. Had the crime scene techs dug over there for some reason?

A chill snaked down his spine. Or had the killer returned?

"Alexis? We need Denali to search for napoo."

"Why?" She followed his gaze. "Oh no. It looks like someone dug into the ground over there."

"Could be nothing," he said, although he didn't believe it. "Maybe the crime scene techs set up a staging area there."

Alexis looked pale but didn't hesitate to kneel beside her dog. "Are you ready to search? Huh, girl? Search! Search napoo."

Denali licked her chops to get the last crumbs of the cookie bone, then lowered her nose to the ground. He and Alexis followed the K9 down the slope to the grave site.

Griff hoped he was wrong. That the darker area of ground wasn't a grave, but a staging site as he'd suggested. Alexis hung back, giving her K9 room to work. Denali didn't make a beeline for the area in question but sniffed along the ground making a circle around the first grave site.

"Shouldn't we go straight to that area?" he asked after a moment.

"No. If there's a body there, Denali will find it."

Alexis's gaze was glued to her K9. "It's not smart to try to lead the dog to where I want to go. Better she does her thing."

He tried to be patient, but his pulse kicked up as Denali made her way to the dark patch of earth. As they grew closer, it was clear his theory of a staging area was off the mark.

Denali went straight to the edge of the over-turned earth, sniffed for a long moment, then sat and barked.

He closed his eyes for a moment, feeling sure the K9 had found Wendy Evers's body. The idea of using the trail cameras to get a picture of this guy was too late.

8

———————

Alexis felt sick to her stomach, imagining Wendy Evers being buried beneath the dirt. She forced herself to pull Denali's pink piggy from the pack Griff carried. "Good girl, Denali! Good girl!" She tossed the piggy, then took several steps from the grave site.

They were too late. She blinked back tears. They'd done their best, Griff had followed up on the few leads they'd gotten, but that hadn't been good enough.

And now that the killer had buried Wendy Evers here, she wasn't sure he'd be back. Why would he?

Griff came over to stand beside her. "I'm sorry."

She subtly swiped at her tears, then glanced up at him. "You don't need to apologize to me. I feel bad about this too."

"I failed Wendy Evers." Griff's expression reflected his regret. "We came too late."

She hated to see him feeling so down. "Griff, if we hadn't come up with the trail cam idea, we wouldn't be here now." She swallowed hard, then added, "I suspect it was too late to save Wendy anyway. The killer doesn't strike me as the patient type."

"No. His escalation is a sign of losing control." Griff stared at the freshly turned dirt. "I should dig a bit to make sure the victim is Wendy. I trust Denali's nose; someone is down there. We're assuming Wendy, but it could be someone else."

The possibility was horrifying. Could this guy have killed another girl so soon?

Yes, he could have. Anyone who would strangle women, bury them in the wilderness, attempt to poison her dog, and shoot at a fed could do anything.

Griff hung his head for a moment. "I can't believe he made his way back here between the various attempts he made toward you."

"Both of us." She stepped closer, putting a hand on his chest. "This isn't your fault, Griff. The killer did this, not you."

He covered her hand with his. "I failed to find Wendy in time."

Her heart ached for him and for Wendy's grandmother. She moved closer, sliding her arms around his waist to hug him. "You didn't fail. You've been doing everything possible to find him."

Griff froze for a second, then hauled her close, burying his face against her hair. She held him, wishing she could say or do something to make him feel better.

"We're going to find him," she whispered. "At some point, he'll make a mistake, and we'll find him."

She leaned back, tipping her head up to look at him. As before, his gaze clung to hers, then dropped to her mouth. A secret thrill ran through her. When he didn't move, she went up on her tippy toes to kiss him.

The chaste kiss instantly morphed into something more. He crushed her close and deepened their kiss. Logical thought evaporated like mist. Her mind only knew Griff's mouth on hers and his warm embrace.

Denali nudged her, breaking the moment. Griff lifted his head, and she frowned when she noticed the regret there. "I shouldn't have done that."

"I kissed you." Stung by his words, she stepped back and took the piggy from Denali. "But don't worry, it was just a kiss. I don't expect anything from you."

"Alexis." He ran his fingers through his hair. "I

care about you, but I also need to stay focused on finding this guy."

Did that mean she was a distraction? That the awareness sizzling between them wasn't one-sided? She forced a smile. "I understand. There's work to be done. Let's get those cameras mounted."

He looked like he might say something more but then stepped back to shrug out of the backpack. As he pulled the cameras, hammer, and nails from the pack, she walked the area, searching for a good tree to use as a mounting post.

"How about here?" She motioned to a tree that overlooked two of the three gravesites. The first one she'd found was farther from the others.

"I like it." Griff glanced around. "I need a tree stump to stand on."

Denali followed her like a shadow as she searched for something appropriate. When she found one, it was too heavy to lift, so she rolled it toward him.

"I've got it." Griff grunted as he lifted the stump. Five minutes later, he had the camera mounted to the tree. As it was tan, green, and brown camouflage in color, it blended pretty well with the tree trunk.

"I think the second camera should go up on the other side, closest to the first grave." Alexis gestured with her hand.

Griff nodded and hauled his log step stool across

the open field. Once the second camera was mounted, he headed back to the fresh grave.

"I don't have cell service, do you?" He looked up at her from the edge of the dirt.

"No, but the sat phone should be in the pack." She rummaged through the items, finding the phone near the bottom. She turned it on and nodded with satisfaction. "Ready to go."

"Thanks." He dug through the dirt with gloved hands. The grave was so fresh it was easy to sift the dirt away to expose the body. It was a young woman.

Her stomach rolled, and when Griff brushed the dirt away from the face, Alexis had to look away.

"It's Wendy." He sounded sad. "Looks as if she was strangled like the others."

Alexis toed the satellite phone. "Make the call. We'll have to stick around here until the crime scene techs show up."

Griff removed his gloves and reached for the phone. She scanned their surroundings but didn't see anything alarming.

Denali would alert her if the guy was close. Although earlier, she hadn't done that because the wind had been coming in from the opposite direction.

That made her wonder if the killer was a wildlife hunter. Maybe he knew all about keeping the wind in his face to avoid being scented by game animals.

She turned to face the wind. Then she decided she should use Denali to make sure this guy hadn't stayed nearby. She knelt beside her K9. "Search, Denali. Search bad guy!"

Denali's tail wagged, and she turned to lower her nose to the ground. Her K9 trotted toward the newly dug grave. Alexis decided to let her alert there again, before asking her to search again.

Rewards kept the K9 excited about the search game.

"Good girl!" She tossed the pink piggy up into the air. "Good girl, Denali."

"Didn't she already alert here?" Griff asked.

"Yes, but now she's tracking the killer's scent verses searching for napoo." After a few minutes of playtime, Alexis extended her arm. "Hand." When Denali regurgitated the piggy into her palm, she paused to pull a water bottle and the collapsible bowl from the pack. Denali lapped the water, then gazed up at her expectantly. "Search! Search bad guy."

If the killer was nearby, Denali would find him. Griff made several phone calls as she followed Denali. The terrain was rough in some places, but she gamely kept up with her K9. Denali leaped over a fallen log, then stopped and sniffed along the base. She sat and barked.

"He was here, huh, girl?" She praised her dog but didn't offer the piggy yet. The fallen log over-looked the most recent gravesite, but there wasn't a direct line of sight to the other two.

Had the killer sat here to rest after burying Wendy Evers?

She took a moment to examine the ground. The earth was hard packed due to lack of rain and re-vealed nothing that would help identify him.

"Search! Search bad guy!"

Denali eagerly went back to work. Rays of sun-light beat down on them. Rivulets of sweat rolled down her face and her back.

After several minutes, Denali stopped near an open area, sniffed, then alerted.

Alexis frowned, as this was a different location from before. She crossed over to see what Denali had found.

At first, she didn't notice anything, but then she saw them. A partial tire print in the dirt. Lowering to a crouch, she examined the marks more closely. She realized they were similar to tracks left by an ATV.

The Sullivans had several four-wheeler ATVs, along with snow machines and horses. Depending on the time of the year and the location of the search, they'd used various methods of travel.

She slowly rose and rewarded Denali for the find. It made sense that the killer had transported the bodies via an all-terrain vehicle. It was something they should have considered sooner. Carrying a dead body all the way into the woods wasn't practical.

"Here, Denali. Hand." She waited for Denali to lope back to give her the piggy. Then she quickly headed back to where Griff remained at the gravesite with Denali at her heels.

She didn't really think the tire track would help find their killer, but it was a piece of the puzzle.

They needed all the help they could get.

GRIFF FINISHED HIS CALLS, feeling more frustrated than ever. The crime scene techs and local law enforcement officials were on their way. That was fine. Then his boss informed him that the FBI profiler's flight had been delayed. She wouldn't be in Wyoming until late evening.

Meanwhile, this brutal killer was searching for another victim. Or worse, coming up with a new plan to grab Alexis.

"Griff!" Alexis ran toward him. "I found a tire track in the woods."

"Tire track?" Realization dawned. "A four-wheeler?"

"Yes. Come with me. It's not much of one, but it looks similar to the ATVs we use for search and rescue missions."

He took a moment to shove the sat phone into the backpack, then stood. Settling the pack on his shoulders, he crossed to her. "Show me."

She nodded. Denali led the way, as if knowing their destination. He hadn't paid much attention to Alexis and Denali combing the area. Ignoring the twinge in his knee, he quickened his pace to catch up.

"Here." Alexis knelt beside the track.

He used his phone to take pictures. "This makes me think he has a place in Greybull or somewhere close by."

"I was thinking about that too." Alexis frowned. "We've been focused on Greybull because that's where Wendy went missing. But the town of Shell isn't that far. It's way smaller, but not having a large population may work to his advantage."

He gave her an admiring look. "That's a good point. There are probably other small towns that are barely a dot on the map as well. However, that doesn't explain his taking victims from Jackson and Casper."

"Maybe he's a truck driver," Alexis suggested.

"Or has a sales job that forces him to travel across the state."

"Those are good possibilities." He shook his head wearily. "I wish we had more to go on. Having fingerprints that aren't in the system isn't helpful."

"That eliminates anyone who has been in the military, law enforcement, or a government job." Alexis sighed. "That doesn't help, as most of the people in Wyoming have never worked in any of those professions."

"I'm aware." Running federal investigations in Wyoming had many disadvantages. Between the weather, the spread-out communities, and the wilderness, he often felt as if closing cases took forever.

And Wendy Evers had paid the price.

He gestured toward the gravesite. "The crime scene techs and local police are on the way. So is the medical examiner. I'm not sure if Dr. Klem has finished the autopsies of the first two victims." He'd intended to stop by to get the results for himself, but the shooting at the hotel had interrupted his plan.

"That's good they'll be here soon." Alexis made her way through the woods to a fallen log. "Denali alerted here, but I don't see anything that resembles evidence."

Griff knelt to inspect the ground. It was covered

with fallen leaves, twigs, and a smattering of pine needles. "I don't see anything either."

"You can see the third grave from here." Alexis dropped down onto the log. Denali stretched out on the ground beside her. "I believe he sat here to rest and admire his work."

Griff nodded. "Then he rode his four-wheeler out of here." He abruptly straightened. "We'll need to get back to the campground. Maybe someone noticed a man putting an ATV on a trailer."

"That sounds like a possibility." She gazed up at him, and for a moment, he was lost in the memory of their kiss. Then he shook it off as she added, "I can't imagine there are many four-wheelers in the campground. I'm sure someone riding it would have been noticed."

He wanted to head out immediately to begin interviewing campers, but they needed to wait until the local police arrived. It would be nice to talk to the medical examiner too.

Hurry and wait, he thought with a sigh.

He joined Alexis on the fallen log. No sense in standing around. They could keep an eye on the gravesite and were protected from the sun by the tree canopy overhead.

"Water?" Alexis offered a half-finished bottle.

"Thanks." He drank, leaving the last quarter for her. "I hope the deputies get here soon."

"They will." She finished the water and carefully tucked the empty bottle in the pack. "They're familiar with the area this time."

"Yeah." They sat in silence for a few minutes. Then he caught movement from across the field. He shot to his feet and narrowed his gaze. "I think they've arrived."

"Great." She rose, and Denali jumped to her feet too. They crossed the field just as deputies Paul Holland and Cameron Newton emerged from the woods.

"Sorry to drag you out here again," Griff said by way of greeting. He gestured to the gravesite. "We found Wendy Evers over there."

"A fresh grave this time," Cameron said. "Considering we were here most of the day and into the evening, he must have done this in the dark."

"That's my assessment," Griff agreed. "And we know he showed up at the Greybull hotel at three in the morning. That narrows the time frame even more."

"The hotel?" Paul frowned.

"Denali alerted us to his scent," Alexis said. "He fired at us and escaped. She tracked his scent to a dead-end road where we assume he had a car waiting."

Paul and Cameron exchanged looks. "You didn't call it in?"

Griff shook his head. "There's no reason to wake everyone up. The lab was able to lift fingerprints from the shell casings but didn't get any hits when they ran them through the system." He shrugged. "We still don't have much to go on."

"We did find a tire track from an ATV," Alexis said. "Denali alerted there, so I believe the killer used that to bring his victims here to bury."

"I should have thought of that," Paul said with a frown.

"Me too," Griff agreed. "I'm heading back to the campground parking lot. I'm going to talk to the campers there. If this guy brought a four-wheeler in, someone may remember seeing him."

Cameron nodded. "That's a good idea."

"I need you guys to stay here until the crime scene techs and medical examiner arrive." Griff was itching to start the canvass.

"Okay by me." Paul glanced to the now-exposed gravesite. "You're sure that's Wendy Evers?"

"Yes." Griff's stomach clenched as he thought of how he'd failed Wendy. And her grandmother. "I'm sure."

"Hey, it's not your fault." Paul slapped him on the back. "We're all doing the best we can with the information we have."

"I know." Logically, Griff knew the deputy was

right. Emotionally? The taste of failure was bitter on his tongue.

"We're going to find him, Griff." Alexis patted his arm. "Let's hike back to the campground."

"I'm ready." He could always talk to the ME later. Following up on this potential lead was more important.

He set a brisk pace, hoping they hadn't missed their window of opportunity by not interviewing the campers sooner. Hopefully there were several who'd been there for a few days or longer.

They passed the halfway point when his phone rang. Obviously, they'd gotten within cell service. He didn't recognize the number but answered it anyway. "Agent Flannery."

"Agent Flannery, this is Dr. Marybeth Klem. I've just arrived at the scene, where are you?" The ME sounded annoyed.

"I'm following up on a lead to our killer, otherwise I would have stayed to talk to you." He realized she must be using a satellite phone and glanced at his watch. "I'm sorry, but it's going to be a while before I can get back there."

"A lead is good, I guess." Dr. Klem backed off. "I wanted to share my preliminary report on the first two victims. I won't have the final report ready until the tox screens come back, which could take up to thirty days."

He was familiar with the delay on toxicology results. Didn't mean he liked it. "Can you email the reports?"

"I can but let me give you the Cliffs Notes version." She paused, then continued. "Both women were sexually assaulted, then strangled to death. Unfortunately, the killer used protection. And I also didn't find skin cells or blood under the victims' fingernails, which makes me think he drugged them so they couldn't fight back. The tox screen will tell us more."

Griff swallowed hard. He'd suspected the girls were sexually assaulted, but hearing the words struck deep. If he could have found Wendy in time . . . but he hadn't. He cleared his throat. "Sounds like our perp is smart enough to minimize DNA."

"Not as smart as he thinks," Dr. Klem said. "We found some hair fibers and will send those for DNA testing. I've asked for the results to be rushed, but I suspect it will still take a few days."

A few days sounded good, but who knew how many girls this guy might grab during that time frame. If the killer didn't get close to Alexis would he settle for someone else? Griff didn't know. "We lifted prints off shell casings, but they didn't match anyone in the system," Griff told her. "We may have better success with DNA, but I won't hold my breath."

"I'm sorry to hear that. Still, you never know." Dr. Klem sounded hopeful. "We may be able to use one of those DNA sites used to find ancestors."

"I'm happy to go that route once we get the results." Griff ducked under a low-hanging tree branch. "Thanks for the update. I'm sorry I couldn't stick around."

"That's okay. Anything you can do to find this guy. I have a thirteen-year-old daughter. The thought of something happening to her..."

"I know. Trust me, I want this guy as badly as you do." Probably more, Griff silently added. His gaze landed on Alexis walking beside Denali. He couldn't bear the idea of this guy getting his hands on her. "Send me the autopsy reports and let me know about the DNA and tox screen."

"Of course." Klem paused, then said, "I'm sorry to learn about the third victim."

It was hard to speak around the lump in his throat. "Me too."

Klem ended the call. Griff pocketed his phone and hurried to catch up to Alexis. The flash of chrome bumpers through the foliage indicated they were close to the campground parking lot.

He quickened his pace, ignoring the way his

knee protested. Maybe later he'd dig the ibuprofen from the backpack.

As they reached the parking lot, a family of four headed toward an SUV. Two parents and two kids one male, one female who appeared to be early teens.

Griff decided he'd start with them. He jogged toward them, the pack bouncing uncomfortably on his back. "Excuse me? Can I have a moment?" He held up his FBI badge. "I need to ask a couple of questions."

"FBI?" The father of the kids appeared to be in his mid-forties. "I've never talked to the FBI before."

"Is there a problem?" The woman stepped closer to the kids.

"No problem. I'm wondering if any of you have seen a man with a four-wheeler." Griff didn't want to spread panic through the campsite. "He was probably here over the past few days."

"Is he a suspect in a crime?" the woman asked fearfully.

"I just want to talk to him," Griff said. In his periphery, he noticed Alexis and Denali had moved close enough to hear the conversation without being intrusive.

"I'm sorry, but I haven't seen him," the man replied. "Have you, Sheri?"

"No, I haven't." Sheri looked thoughtful. "I may

have heard a four-wheeler, but it could have been a car."

The engine of an ATV was much smaller than a car, but Griff nodded. He was about to pull out a business card, when the boy said, "I saw him."

Sheri whirled to look at her son. "Tim, are you sure? When did you see a four-wheeler?"

Tim glanced up at his father, then shrugged. "Okay, you won't like this, but Darla and I took a walk late last night. We came this way for privacy."

Tim's mother looked like she might faint. "Tim! You're too young to be dating!"

Tim rolled his eyes. "It wasn't a date. We just wanted a quiet place to talk."

"To talk or make out?" Sheri demanded.

Griff held up his hand. As much as he appreciated Sheri's concern for her son, he needed information. "Go on, Tim. Tell me about the four-wheeler."

"Oh yeah. Well, Darla and I heard a rumbling sound. We stopped and waited, thinking someone was pulling into the parking lot." Tim flushed beneath his mother's piercing gaze. "We didn't do anything," he said defensively. Then to Griff, he said, "I realized the engine wasn't a car, but a small motorcycle or ATV. And I was right because just then a guy came riding out of the woods into the parking lot."

Griff's pulse skyrocketed. They had a witness! "Did you get a good look at him?"

Tim grimaced. "Not really. He was about as tall as my dad but way younger. Maybe in his twenties? He had dark hair. He walked to a large Ram pickup truck with a small trailer. He used a ramp to get the ATV into the trailer, and then he drove away."

Griff nodded encouragingly. "You're sure he was driving a Ram pickup truck?"

"Yeah. It was an older model, but it's just like the one I'd like some day." Tim glanced at his parents. "Hey, I'll be sixteen in a year and two months!"

"What about the color of the truck?" Griff asked, before Sheri could interrupt. "Or a license plate?"

Tim shook his head. "I didn't look at the plate. The truck was light in color, but in the dark, it was hard to see. Maybe gray or silver. Could have been a dirty white."

Griff knew there were hundreds of white, silver, or gray Ram trucks in the state. But he could at least get a list to see if any of the names popped. "Is there anything else you can tell me about the driver? Anything specific that you noticed?"

Tim frowned. "Not really. Oh, he wore a baseball cap. Does that help?"

Griff nodded. "Yes, Tim, you've been a great help." He turned to Tim's parents. "Do you mind if I take down your names and phone numbers?"

"I'm Dave Johnson, and this is my wife, Sheri. Our son, Tim, and our daughter, Sylvie."

Griff entered their personal information into his phone. Then he stepped back as the family piled into the car and headed out. No doubt Sheri was giving Tim grief over his late-night walk with Darla.

A man in his twenties wearing a ball cap and driving a white, silver, or gray Ram truck pulling a trailer. It was the first solid lead he'd gotten since this nightmare had started.

For the first time since Grace had passed away, Griff lifted his gaze to the sky and opened his heart to prayer.

Please, Lord Jesus, help me find this man before anyone else gets hurt!

9

———

"Is there a way to find the light-colored Ram truck?" Alexis looked at Griff expectantly. "You must have access to a database that can provide that information."

He nodded and reached for his phone. "I'll call the office now to request DMV records for white, silver, and gray Ram trucks. The list may be long, so this may not help as much as we hope. But it's a starting place for sure."

Large trucks were highly popular in Wyoming. She waited as Griff made the call, stroking Denali's fur as the dog sat beside her. When he finished, she asked, "Do you think there's a chance this guy is from out of state?"

"Anything is possible, but I hope not." Griff

sighed and shifted the pack. "Let's go. We have more people to talk to."

She nodded, surprised they'd gotten so much information from the first family they approached. If not for Tim and Darla's late-night walk, they wouldn't have learned anything new. "Come, Denali."

She and Griff made their way through the campground. Several people mentioned hearing the sound of an engine that could have belonged to the four-wheeler but claimed they didn't see the ATV itself or who was riding it. They found Darla and her parents, who were also not happy to learn of her late-night walk with Tim. Darla was a pretty girl with long dark hair, but as Griff questioned her about the ATV, she couldn't provide anything more than they'd learned from Tim.

"I didn't even know it was a Ram truck," she said.

"Thanks." Griff offered another of his business cards. "If you think of anything else, please let me know."

"And if you see the man riding the ATV again, stay away," Alexis added. "We're concerned he may have hurt another girl."

Darla's mother drew her close. "Thanks for the warning."

Griff nodded, and they moved on. "I'm glad you

mentioned that," he confided when they were out of earshot. "I didn't want to cause alarm, but I should have warned the people here to stay far away from him."

She grimaced. "I'm not sure he'll be back. Even if he didn't notice Tim and Darla in the trees, he won't want to risk coming here again. Especially not once he realizes we've found Wendy Evers's body."

Griff sighed. "You're probably right, although I hope he does come back, or putting up those trail cameras was a fruitless effort." He glanced at his watch. "Let's keep going. We're almost finished covering the campground."

She nodded. Denali was a trouper, staying close and sniffing the air with interest as they passed people cooking over a campfire.

By the time they'd returned to the parking lot, the hour was going on noon. Griff stood for a minute surveying the space. "What are you thinking?" she asked when he didn't say anything for a long moment.

"I was debating taking down license plate numbers to make sure we talk to everyone who was here." He sighed and rubbed the back of his neck. "I'm not sure they'd have any more information, though. And I'm starving. I'd rather head to Shell for lunch."

She nodded. "I agree that Tim and Darla are the

key witnesses. It sounds like they were alone here; their parents didn't even know they were gone."

"Yeah." Griff hesitated, then quickly pulled out his phone. "I'll take pictures of the plates. If the DMV list of Ram trucks doesn't reveal anything to go on, I can reach out to the owners of these cars."

"Okay." As he did that, she opened the rear hatch of the SUV for Denali. Thanks to the July sun, it was hot and stuffy inside, so she opened all four doors too. Then she started the car, cranking the air-conditioning on high.

She gave Denali water, then signaled for the K9 to get in. The interior of the vehicle was tolerable by the time Griff finished. He tossed the backpack onto the floor of the back seat.

"I'll drive if you don't mind." Alexis quickly slid in behind the wheel. "If that list comes through, you can start reviewing it."

"That may take time, but I have the autopsy reports to read." He went around to the passenger side and got in. He peered at his phone as she headed toward Shell. "I hate knowing these girls have been drugged, then assaulted and murdered. This guy is a predator. I need to get him off the street as soon as possible."

She nodded. It had been difficult to look at Wendy Evers's face. Knowing their names made it more personal. "Griff?" When he looked up from his phone, she said, "You need to talk to Wendy's grandmother."

A pained expression creased his face. "I know. We'll head back to Greybull soon. Thankfully, the media hasn't been around yet, but I'm sure that will happen soon enough. I feel the need to check Shell, see if there's any reason to suspect our guy has a place there."

"Sounds good."

Shell was smaller than she'd remembered. Alexis had driven through without paying much attention in the past, but seeing it now, she realized there were probably fewer than a hundred people living there.

As with every small town, there was a restaurant/bar and a gas station. No doubt the town survived on the spattering of tourists who visited the Bighorns in the summer and the hunters who flocked to the area in the fall. As she pulled into the restaurant parking lot, Griff looked up from his phone.

"Wow, this place is tiny, huh?" He looked disappointed.

"Yep." She opened the back hatch for Denali and slid out of the seat. "If we had a better description of this guy, we'd probably be able to rule this place out. I'm sure the residents here know each other pretty well."

Griff sighed and joined her behind the SUV. Denali stretched, then stood with her nose up, sniffing the air. "I guess this is a wasted trip. I don't see a Ram truck, and I doubt this guy is sitting inside the restaurant. I'm too hungry to head back to Greybull without eating."

She glanced at her K9, then reached into the back seat for the piggy. "Let's see if Denali alerts on his scent." She hunkered down near the dog. "Are you ready to search? Huh, girl? Search bad guy!"

Denali eagerly went to work, sniffing the parking lot, then trotting toward the door. Alexis knew that even if her K9 alerted on the killer's scent, that didn't mean this was his home base. It only meant he'd been here recently.

Her K9 sniffed at the corner of the parking lot, then sat and barked. Alexis was surprised but quickly went over to praise her dog. "Good girl!" She tossed the piggy into the air. "Good girl, Denali."

Griff watched Denali run around with the pink piggy in her mouth. "What's your thought on how recently this guy was here? Hours? Days?"

"I'd say twenty-four hours, give or take a few." She stared at the ground. "Scent particles can linger on the ground. Based on this alert, I'm thinking she alerted on drops of his sweat or maybe his saliva if he spit."

"Okay." Griff gestured to the door. "Let's see if anyone will tell us if they've seen a light-colored Ram truck recently. I'll pretend I backed into it and am trying to find the owner to pay for damages."

She arched a brow. "Okay, but out here, people don't fix minor dents and dings."

"I'll pretend I'm from Colorado, where people are more civilized." His tone was teasing, so she didn't take offense.

After getting the piggy from Denali, they headed inside. There were a handful of people seated within the restaurant and a few more at the bar. A plump woman in her fifties with gray-streaked hair pulled into a bun appeared to be taking orders and serving meals. She waved them in. "Have a seat."

"Thanks." There were no booths, so she picked a table away from the others. Denali stretched out at her feet and promptly fell asleep. The poor dog had worked hard.

The menu was limited to sandwiches and pizza, but that was okay. Griff didn't seem to mind either.

"My name is Ellen. What can I get you to drink?"

"Water for me, thanks," Alexis said.

"I'll have a Coke," Griff added. "And if you don't mind, we'd like to place our food order."

"Go ahead." Ellen pulled out her notepad.

"I'll have the cheeseburger." Alexis smiled to put the woman at ease. "Thank you. We haven't eaten since really early this morning."

"I'll have a cheeseburger too," Griff said. "By the way, do you know if anyone here drives a light-colored Dodge Ram pickup truck? I struck one, but the guy took off before I could offer to pay for the damages. He's a younger guy, maybe in his twenties? Wears a baseball cap?"

Ellen flipped her notebook shut. "Gotta say that describes a lot of people who pass through. I don't pay attention to their cars, though. Sorry." She moved away. "I'll get your orders in."

"Do you think she's being vague on purpose?" Griff asked.

She shrugged. "Why would she?"

"I don't know." Griff sighed again. "It's my nature to be suspicious. Since Ellen doesn't seem to know cars, I'll ask the guys at the bar when we leave."

"Where did you grow up?" Alexis realized she didn't know much about Griff's personal life. He'd mentioned his wife's passing, but she had assumed he'd grown up in the area.

"Phoenix, Arizona. I went to college at the university and worked for the local police department before applying for a position in the FBI." He cocked his head. "I was kidding about Colorado. Although I will say things are different in Wyoming. Less civilized in some ways."

"I've heard this isn't a post most agents want."

"I don't mind. I like hunting and fishing. Not that I get as much time off for recreational activities." He sat back in his seat as Ellen brought their drinks. "Thanks." He downed half his soft drink in one long gulp.

"We've always lived here," Alexis said. "My older siblings were spread across the state until my parents died. They came back to the ranch for Trevor's and Kendra's sake. Maya had the idea of doing search and rescue." She reached beneath the table to pet Denali. "I'm glad. Not only did this profession keep us closer together as a family, but I like knowing we're providing a service to the community."

"A valuable service." Griff smiled. "From the moment I was assigned here, your family was all I heard about."

She flushed and sipped her water. "I guess we've made a name for ourselves."

"You have." He stopped talking when Ellen brought their plates. "Looks great, thanks."

Alexis smiled, then reached for Griff's hand. "I'd like to say grace."

He nodded and bowed his head. She understood why his faith had stumbled; it wasn't easy to move on after losing someone you loved. "Dear Lord Jesus, we ask You to continue to guide us to seek this evil man who harms others. Please grant us the strength and wisdom we need to find him. Amen."

"Amen." Griff's fingers tightened on hers for a moment before he withdrew. "Thanks, Alexis. I hope we are able to find him soon."

Their burgers were good, and they ate in silence. Alexis was surprised her appetite had returned. She wasn't sure how Griff handled the violent crimes he investigated.

Not that searching disaster sites with Denali for victims was easy.

When they finished, she headed for the restroom with Denali on her heels. When she emerged, she saw Griff was already at the bar, chatting with the customers. He crossed over to join her. "Nobody knows anyone living in the area with a light-colored Ram truck, and the town is small enough that they would."

"Maybe he lives in Greybull after all." She started the SUV remotely as they walked toward it.

"I need to talk to Barbara Evers," Griff said, his expression grim. "After that, we'll go over the list of light-colored Ram trucks."

"Okay." The description was their best lead.

Everyone in Wyoming drove trucks, vans, or SUVs. The weather made them a necessity. But the state also wasn't as highly populated as Colorado or others. Maybe they would find something to go on.

They quickly covered the distance between Shell and Greybull. Griff gave her directions to Barbara Evers's home. When she pulled into the driveway, she noticed an older woman peeking out the window.

"Wait here." Griff pushed out of the car and strode to the front door. Barbara had already opened it and stepped out. The hopeful expression on her face collapsed as Griff spoke. Then she was sobbing into her hands. Griff pulled her close and patted her back.

Alexis blinked away her tears. Three dead girls and only a vague description of a car and the man responsible to go on.

She closed her eyes and prayed again for strength and guidance.

Giving death notifications was the worst part of the job. Griff had done it more as a cop than in his role within the bureau. Yet he was shocked by the strength of Barbara's faith as she pulled herself together. "Thanks, Griff. I'm going to take some comfort in knowing Wendy is with God now."

"I'm doing everything possible to find this guy."

"I know you are." Barbara offered a watery smile. "Will you let me know when that happens?"

"Of course." That was the least he could do. "Please take care of yourself."

"You be careful too." Barbara patted his arm, then stepped back. "You know, I had a bad feeling she was dead. I didn't want to believe it, but I knew she was gone."

He didn't know what to say, so he simply nodded and turned to head back to the SUV. He drew in a deep steadying breath before opening the door. That Barbara could find peace knowing Wendy was in heaven humbled him.

Maybe it was time for him to accept the idea Grace was in a better place too.

"Are you okay?" Alexis's gaze mirrored concern. "That must have been difficult."

"Barbara Evers shares your faith." He eyed the small house as Alexis backed out of the driveway. "She's dealing with the loss better than I could have imagined."

"Faith and prayer can ease the grief," Alexis murmured. "We leaned on our faith after losing our parents, but that doesn't mean we didn't miss them.

Barbara will miss her granddaughter for a long time."

He nodded, tearing his gaze from the Evers's home. "I hope I can figure out a way to narrow that list of trucks."

"We will." She sounded confident, but he wasn't convinced. Checking his phone, he grimaced when he didn't see the email yet. Being back in Greybull was unsettling. It was only a few hours ago that the killer had tried to poison Denali.

Was he still in the area? "Keep your eye out for big trucks."

"I've noticed two black Ram trucks." She glanced at him. "They're rather distinctive, aren't they?"

"Yeah, that's the one thing in our favor." He scanned the vehicles as she drove through town. "As much as I'd like to keep driving around, we need a hotel. I want to print the truck list when I get it. That way we can both look it over."

"We could go back to the hotel where we spent the night. Could be our guy won't expect us to return there."

Griff mulled over that for a moment. It wasn't as if they had many options. Maybe she was right that the killer would think they'd avoid the place. "Okay, that works."

Alexis drove through town, past the campground and the hardware store. There were more vehicles out and about, and when he caught sight of a large Ram truck sitting in the parking lot of the Attwell Restaurant, he grasped her arm. "Turn in there."

She hit the brake and made the turn. The truck looked new, which didn't match the description provided by Tim Johnson. Yet it had been dark, close to midnight. Maybe the kid had made a mistake.

Then he noticed the vehicle didn't have a trailer hitch. Still, he decided to call in the plate number. "I need to know who this truck is registered to. Name, age, and residence." He rattled off the plate number. After a few seconds, he had his answer.

"That truck is registered to Gerald Harp, age sixty-three from Cody. Does that help?"

"Only that we can rule him out. Thanks." He lowered the phone. "False alarm on my part. This isn't our guy. Keep going."

Alexis nodded and made a turn in the parking lot of the restaurant. They passed a couple of other Ram trucks, but they weren't the right color.

Hopefully, Tim Johnson hadn't been wrong about that, he thought grimly.

The clerk at the hotel agreed to give them the same room back, mostly because the housekeeping staff hadn't gotten around to cleaning it. "We've had several rooms turn over today. Suites aren't in high demand."

"We'll take it without being cleaned, thanks." He paid for another night, then led the way down the hall. Alexis and Denali followed.

Denali sniffed the room for a few minutes, then settled down as if recognizing they'd been there before. *Smart dog*, he thought. Alexis's K9 was their best chance of finding the killer.

He only hoped Alexis and Denali wouldn't get hurt in the process.

"There's one way we can draw this guy out of hiding." Alexis dropped onto the sofa. Denali curled up at her feet. "He wants me, right?"

"No." Griff was shocked she'd suggested it. "I'm not placing you in harm's way."

"Take a moment and think it through." Her voice was calm. "I trust you to keep me safe, and we can use local law enforcement as backup. My biggest concern is Denali." She frowned as she bent to stroke her dog. "I don't want to send her back to the ranch, but I don't want her to get hurt either."

"No," he repeated. She was worried about the dog? He didn't want this killer anywhere near Alexis. "We'll find him using good old-fashioned police work." He stared at his phone, willing the list of vehicles to pop up on the screen. "There's no reason to use you or anyone else as bait."

"Why not? You'd rather some other girl be taken against her will?" She shot him an exasperated look. "You want to find another dead body in his burial site?"

"No, but I don't think he's looking for anyone else." Griff held her gaze. "We both know he's focused on you. Maybe he is someone you know from Cody or from somewhere else. Maybe he delivered supplies to your ranch at some point."

She sighed. "I hadn't thought of the delivery angle. We've had plenty of supplies delivered over the past few months. Maybe he has been at the ranch. Unfortunately, I don't see how that helps us find him."

"Can you get records of those deliveries?" Griff wasn't entirely convinced this guy had been on the ranch, but it was another angle to pursue.

He didn't dare ignore a potential lead.

His phone rang, jarring him from his thoughts. "Flannery."

"Griff? It's Sue in the lab. I have the results on the dog food that was brought in an hour ago."

He wondered how the Sullivan twins had gotten the evidence to Cheyene so quickly. Likely Logan had made the trip via plane. He really needed to reimburse the guy for fast-tracking his investigation. "What did you find?"

"The dog food was laced with arsenic. I believe a

highly toxic brand of rat poison was used. Not a lot, but it would have been enough to kill the dog." Sue hesitated, then asked, "Was one of the Sullivan dogs targeted?"

"Yes. Thanks for the information, I'll pass it along."

"I hope you get him, Griff." Sue sounded upset. "Bad enough he's killing women, but dogs too? The Sullivans helped my sister find her son when he got lost in the woods. I can't believe anyone living in the area would target them."

"I know, it's not a good situation, but I'll find him." Griff strove to sound confident. "Thanks again, Sue." He lowered the phone. "You were right. The dog food was laced with arsenic, likely from rat poison."

Alexis nodded. "I knew it would be something like that. Although I don't know who would have that type of rat poison around. Maybe the hardware store?" She jumped to her feet. "We should check. See if the clerk remembers anyone buying any today. I can't imagine it's an item that's purchased often."

"That's a good idea." He grinned. "You're starting to think like a cop."

"That's what happens when you work with siblings who are in law enforcement. Come, Denali."

The trip to the hardware store didn't take long. It

was fairly busy, and they had to wait in line before they could talk to a clerk. Griff flashed his badge. "I need to know if anyone bought highly toxic rat poison today."

"Not while I was here but let me call the manager." The clerk turned, and yelled, "Tony? The FBI wants to talk to you."

Customers turned and stared, making Griff wince. He moved to stand next to Alexis and Denali so those behind him could pay for their purchases.

"FBI?" An older man came over, his expression alarmed. "Why do you want to talk?"

"You're not in trouble, but I'd like to know if anyone purchased toxic rat poison today." Griff tried to look reassuring. "We're following up on some poison found at a nearby campsite."

Tony frowned. "I'm surprised something like that would bring the FBI here. To be honest, I had some rat poison stolen early this morning. I was in the back when I heard the door open. Less than a minute later, I heard the door again. I didn't think much about it, but when I went through the aisles straightening items, I noticed the empty space and realized a box was missing."

Griff ground his teeth in frustration. He hadn't anticipated the killer would have stolen the poison. "What time was that?"

"Like five minutes past nine." Tony looked from

Griff to Alexis. "I still don't understand why the FBI is involved."

"Did you notice a truck or some other vehicle in the parking lot?" Griff pressed, avoiding his question. "Anything that might help us find him?"

"I didn't call the local police to report the theft." Tony frowned. "I hate to say it, but shoplifting isn't uncommon. And no, I didn't see a car. I don't have cameras either."

Griff tried not to show his disappointment. "Here's my card. If you think of anything else, please call me. We appreciate your time."

"Sure." Tony still looked perplexed as they left.

"Another dead end," Alexis murmured as they climbed back into the SUV.

"Yeah." His phone rang again, and his boss's name flashed on the screen. Were they having trouble getting the list of trucks from the DMV? He quickly answered. "Flannery."

"I just got a report of another missing girl. We've issued an Amber alert." As his boss spoke, his phone buzzed with the emergency alert. "Her name is Maureen Kaufman, seventeen years old, taken from the campground in Greybull." A pause, then, "That's where you are, right?"

"Yes, I'm very close to the campground in Greybull. Send me her information and a way to contact her parents. I'll get right on it." Griff lowered the phone, feeling sick as he looked at the photo of the girl who'd gone missing. Or more likely had been taken against her will.

His theory of the killer being focused on Alexis had been proven wrong. The killer had struck again.

And he couldn't bear the thought of being too late to save Maureen the way he'd failed Wendy Evers.

"W

hat happened?" Alexis stared at Griff in concern. He'd gone pale and his expression was grim. "You look upset."

"There's a missing seventeen-year-old girl from the Greybull campground. Maureen Kaufman." He raked his hand through his hair, then reached over to start the engine. "I can't believe the killer struck so close to where he left the poisoned dog food."

"He wants our attention." The burger she'd eaten earlier roiled in her stomach. She hadn't anticipated this. She'd mentally prepared herself to be used as bait to draw him out. Now some other young girl was in danger. "Maybe he's goading us into tracking him down."

"If that's the case, he'll get his wish." His phone

dinged. He glanced at the screen, enlarging the photo that had come through via a text message. He turned it so she could see Maureen's picture. She was a pretty girl, reddish hair and freckles that made her look younger than seventeen. Interestingly, Maureen didn't look anything like his previous victims. Then again, they'd all been physically different.

"I'm sure he grabbed Maureen as a crime of opportunity." She held Griff's gaze. "But I thought most serial killers had some sort of pattern to their victims. Either they looked alike or had a similar profession. I don't understand how his victims are related."

"I don't either. That's something the FBI profiler is supposed to help us understand." Griff backed out of the parking lot and drove toward the campground practically across the street. "I can't believe this," he muttered as he saw a couple hugging each other and another teenage girl huddling beside them. "Those must be her parents, Beth and Nate Kaufman. The information from my boss didn't include a sibling."

"Open the back hatch. I'm coming with you." Alexis would use Denali to track the bad guy's scent. She wished now that Joel and his K9 Royal were here to track Maureen's scent. But she didn't bother to call him. In theory, the two scents would be on the same path.

Was it possible Maureen hadn't been taken by their killer?

She grabbed the backpack from the floorboards of the rear seat. She wasn't sure how far this guy had taken Maureen, but it was always better to be prepared.

Griff crossed to the upset couple and showed them his badge. Shouldering the pack, she hurried over to listen to the conversation. Denali jumped out of the back, stretched, then trotted over to stand beside her.

"I don't know what time she went missing," Nate Kaufman was saying. "The girls have their own tent, and we have ours. Lindsey didn't realize Maureen had gotten up."

Griff turned toward Lindsey. "Did your sister often get up in the middle of the night? Or was this a first-time thing?"

"I don't know." Lindsey sniffed and her red, puffy eyes indicated she'd been crying. "I don't think she did that before. She's always been there when I woke up except for today. I crawled out of bed and walked around trying to find her. I figured she was hanging out with some of the other kids, so I walked the entire campsite looking for her. I was afraid to tell Mom and Dad at first, but then I was really worried." Lindsey swiped at her face. "Maureen was eating one of the cinnamon buns Dad picked up yesterday, though. There's a partially squashed one near the picnic table that wasn't there before." Fresh tears welled in Lindsey's eyes. "I didn't know she woke up and left the tent. I didn't know!"

Alexis's heart went out to the young girl. Griff noticed her distress as well.

"This isn't your fault, Lindsey." His tone was soothing as he rested a hand on the girl's slim shoulder. "Can you tell me if Maureen met anyone here? Maybe a boy she wanted to sneak out to meet up with?"

The conversation they'd had with Tim Johnson who'd gone out to meet Darla flashed in her mind. Teenagers were walking bundles of raging hormones. The possibility of Maureen sneaking out to meet someone was legitimate.

"Maureen doesn't have a boyfriend," Beth Kaufman said.

"She doesn't, but Maureen did hang out with a guy named Simon. He left with his parents yesterday." Lindsey sniffled again. "Maureen said he was from Jackson. We live in Cheyenne, so I don't think they'll see each other again."

"Simon who?" Nate demanded.

His wife looked equally confused. "Why didn't Maureen tell me about this boy?"

Ah, the joys of parenting teenagers, Alexis thought. They were always the last to know.

Lindsey shook her head. "I don't know why she didn't say anything. And I didn't ask his last name."

"We need to know his last name!" Nate barked with a flash of anger. "I want to talk to his parents."

"I don't know! Chill out, Dad. It wasn't a big deal. They weren't kissing or anything like that. They were just friends." Lindsey waved toward the parking lot. "Simon left yesterday. Maureen walked him here to the parking lot. I saw them hugging each other, but that was it. He left, and that was the end of it."

Griff exchanged a look with Alexis, and she knew he was wondering if they were on the wrong track assuming the killer had abducted Maureen. Maybe Simon wasn't the only boy Maureen had befriended. There could be others.

There was only one way to know for sure. She gestured to Denali, and Griff nodded, silently agreeing with her plan.

He turned to the Kaufmans. "We'd like to see your campsite."

The couple nodded and turned to lead the way. Their campsite was situated far away from the others and near the back of the campground. Standing near the now-doused campfire, Alexis couldn't see any neighboring tents nearby. The isolation may have contributed to the killer's ability to kidnap Maureen.

If that's who'd taken her.

Lindsey eyed Denali curiously. "Is your dog specially trained?"

"Yes, she is. But don't worry, she never bites." Alexis removed the backpack, filled a collapsible bowl with water, and offered it to Denali. Her border collie lapped the water, then lifted her head, dark-brown eyes curious. Alexis ruffled Denali's fur. "Are you ready to work? Huh, girl? Search! Search bad guy."

Beth gasped in horror at her words. Alexis felt bad for scaring the woman, but she needed to use the same term she had before. Denali was a cadaver dog, so she didn't want to confuse the K9 by calling their bad guy something else.

"We're not sure a bad guy took your daughter," Griff quickly explained as Denali lowered her nose to sniff the area. "We're taking precautions."

Denali sniffed past the bigger of the two tents, then went to the fire pit and buried her nose in the grass. Her K9 sat and barked sharply.

Her alert. Their killer had definitely been there. Doing her best not to show her concern, Alexis pulled the pink piggy from the backpack and joined her K9. She noticed the smashed cinnamon roll in the grass and tried not to imagine Maureen fighting for her life as the assailant grabbed her. "Good girl. Search! Search bad guy."

"What does that mean?" Mrs. Kaufman said, her voice escalating. "Did the dog find something? Was our daughter taken by a bad guy?"

"I don't know yet, we're still investigating." Griff was vague, no doubt wanting more time before he had to tell them the truth. "We need to let them work, okay?"

Alexis continued to follow Denali as her K9 tracked the bad guy's scent. She wasn't surprised when Denali headed to a path that led into the woods. It made sense that the killer would have taken his victim out this way to avoid being seen.

Or heard. She thought about what Griff had said about the girls being drugged. Did he use something on them during the abduction to keep them quiet? Hard to imagine as most drugs took at least a few minutes to work.

Unless he used something old-fashioned like chloroform. Alexis had no idea if chloroform was still around and available for purchase. Maybe that was something they should investigate, too.

Denali picked up her pace. It was obvious her K9 had the bad guy's scent imprinted on her mind.

She heard Griff following behind her but didn't look back. She didn't want to lose sight of Denali. It was hard to imagine the bad guy being up ahead waiting for them to emerge. If he was smart, he'd be far away from here. Yet after the poisoned dog food incident, she wasn't putting anything past him.

After a few minutes, she noticed Denali slowed her pace. The K9 still had her nose to the ground, so Alexis didn't think she'd lost the scent. Denali paused, lifted her nose, then jumped over a fallen log. The K9 didn't alert, though. As if the log was nothing, her K9 kept trotting along, following the scent.

The bad guy must have gone over the log too. Had he carried Maureen over it? How had he kept the girl quiet?

"Alexis?" Griff's voice floated to her. "Everything okay?"

"Yes. Denali is on it." She flashed a reassuring smile over her shoulder, then continued after her dog.

Griff caught up with her a minute later. "The parents are wrecked."

"I don't blame them." She didn't envy his job of letting them know their daughter had likely been abducted by a serial killer.

"I called my boss, told him to have the profiler call me the minute she lands." He shook his head. "I just can't believe he struck so close to his previous victim. I'm worried he's losing control."

"He's emotionally disturbed." She frowned

when Denali disappeared through the trees. Breaking into a run, the backpack jostling with every step, she closed the gap.

"Denali?" She was suddenly afraid something had happened. But as soon as she broke through the trees, she slowed. Denali was there, sniffing along a dirt road.

Then her K9 sat and barked.

Alexis crossed over to her dog. "Good girl, Denali! Good girl!" She tossed the pink piggy behind her to keep the dog from messing up any potential evidence.

"Is this the end of the trail?" Griff joined her near the road.

"Yes." Dropping to a crouch, she examined the ground. There hadn't been any rain recently, but she could still make out the barest image of a tire track. She glanced at Griff, who'd knelt beside her. "Is it possible this belongs to a Ram truck?"

"I'm not a tire expert, but we can hope it's a match." Griff took pictures with his phone, then fiddled around with it for a few minutes.

She straightened, watching Denali play. She felt sad, angry, and full of despair over Maureen's abduction. And other than the light-colored Ram truck, they had nothing to go on to find this guy.

They were running out of time to rescue Maureen. The only idea she could come up with was to use herself as a lure to draw him out. And now that there was another missing girl's life on the line, she would not accept no as an answer.

GRIFF HAD FOUND the tires that were typically used on Ram trucks, and to his inexpert eye, they matched the track Denali had found. He'd need the lab to tell him for sure.

Even that wasn't something he could use in court. Not unless they found the actual truck used in the abductions. There was always the possibility the owner of the truck had changed the tires to a brand that wasn't standard. Out here, tires needed to be replaced more frequently than those driving in the city.

He turned as Alexis and Denali joined him. Alexis had the pink piggy in hand. Under different circumstances, he'd have smiled at the way she carried Denali's reward.

There was nothing to smile about now. Maureen Kaufman was the serial killer's next victim, and if they didn't figure out who this guy was soon, they'd likely find her dead body.

He drew in a deep breath, fighting to remain calm. He couldn't let this case get to him on an emotional level. He needed to think like this guy. To figure out who he was. Based on the two most recent abductions being here in Greybull, he leaned toward believing the killer lived here or at least used the town as his home base. He'd taken the other victims from Casper and Jackson.

Simon was also from Jackson, but Griff didn't see him as the killer.

Hopefully, the list of Ram trucks would point them to a suspect. "We need to head back. I need to let the Kaufmans know that we lost the scent trail and that we know there's a serial killer in the area." A pit of dread formed in his stomach. He hated this part of the job. The news would terrify them.

Especially since he didn't have much of a lead. He'd gotten the list of light-colored Ram trucks, so he and Alexis could work on that.

It seemed too little, too late.

He walked in silence for a minute, dreading the conversation looming before him. Then he sighed. "Maureen's abduction is likely to hit the news very soon." He had hoped for more time before the media frenzy descended on the town.

"Will that work against us in finding him?" Alexis asked.

"I don't know." He shrugged. "To be honest, it doesn't matter at this point. Maureen is his fourth victim, unless there are others we don't know about. I'm surprised we've been able to contain the news this long. Some serial killers enjoy the attention. It makes them think they're smarter than the cops and federal agents."

Alexis grimaced as they hopped over the fallen log. "I don't like giving him anything he wants."

"I don't either. But it's time to put the entire state on high alert." He worried the killer was spiraling out of control. The only good news was that being rushed might cause the killer to make mistakes. "Teenage girls need to be careful and stay close to home or make sure they're with friends until we catch him."

"It's not like Maureen wandered away from the campsite." Alexis frowned. "The smashed cinnamon roll tells me he caught her there and somehow managed to get her away without waking up her family."

"I noticed. And I'm not sure how he's managing to get these girls to go along with him." They continued retracing their steps. A few minutes later, the campsite came into view. The minute the Kaufmans noticed they'd returned, the three of them rushed over.

"Did you find anything?" The hope in Beth's expression ripped at his heart.

"Denali followed the scent to a dirt road about a hundred yards from here." He forced himself to hold her gaze. "I'm sorry to say, it appears Maureen's abductor had a truck waiting there."

Beth Kaufman gasped and buried her face in her hands. Her husband stared at him. "You're saying Maureen has been kidnapped?"

"Yes." He cleared his throat. "I'm very sorry, but you need to know there's been three teenage girls who went missing. We've found their dead bodies buried in a field near the Bighorn Mountains. We have reason to believe the same man who killed them has Maureen."

"No, no, no." Beth moaned and began to sob. "This can't be happening."

"I'm sorry," Griff repeated. Lindsey's eyes filled with tears, and she looked as if she was going to break down too. He lightly grasped the girl's arm. "Lindsey, I really need your help. Do you know what a Ram truck looks like? It's big and has the word Ram in the chrome along the front grill." He pulled out his phone and used his thumb to bring up the picture. "Like this. Can you remember seeing something like this in the parking lot when your sister said goodbye to Simon?"

Lindsey swiped at her face and peered down at the screen. After a long moment, she shook her head. "I know there were a couple trucks parked in the lot, but I can't remember if they looked like this one. I mean, I didn't pay attention to if they were Ram trucks or some other kind."

"That's okay, what color were the trucks you saw?" Griff pressed.

"One was gray; the other was black." Lindsey sniffled loudly again. "Are you going to find my sister?"

"I promise I'm going to do everything I can to find her." He pocketed his phone. Nate Kaufman held his wife, his own expression full of anguish.

"How did this happen?" Nate asked. "I don't understand."

"I—we have been searching for him for the past twenty-four hours." Griff couldn't help feeling guilty that they hadn't gone to the press sooner. Would doing so have kept Maureen safe? He swallowed hard. "The first two girls went missing from other cities far from here. The third victim lived in Greybull. We're following up on leads, and I have a profiler flying in from DC very soon."

"My God," Nate whispered.

"My K9 knows his scent," Alexis said, speaking up for the first time. She rested her hand on Denali's head as the dog sat tall at her side. "Denali followed his scent from your campsite all the way to the dirt road. She's super smart, and I trust her ability to follow scents. I'm sure Denali will help us find the man who took your daughter."

Beth lifted her head from her husband's chest, a bit of hope lightening her eyes. "Your K9 knows his scent? You can use her to search every house in town?"

Every house would be impossible, but Griff had no intention of mentioning that. If they had a general area in mind, yes. But they couldn't randomly comb the entire town.

"As Agent Flannery said, we're following up on every possible lead." Alexis gave the Kaufmans a reassuring look. "We won't stop until we find him."

Griff pulled a business card from his pocket. "You can call me anytime. And I'll need your contact information as well."

A few minutes later, Griff led Alexis and Denali back to the parking lot. As she opened the back hatch for Denali, he quickly scanned the vehicles. The black Ram truck was still there. There was no sign of the gray one.

"I have the list of Ram trucks," he told Alexis as they piled into the SUV. "I think we start with those who are in the Greybull area."

"Good idea. We should start with the ones registered to young men." Alexis put the car in gear and pulled out of the parking lot.

"I'm not sure narrowing the list by age of the registered driver is a good idea," Griff said. "What if this guy is driving a truck registered to one of his parents? No, I think we cover each one of them. I'll even recheck the one truck owned by the sixty-three-year-old man."

"I hadn't thought of that," Alexis admitted. "Good plan. Once we find them, I'll have Denali search the area nearby to see if she alerts."

"I was hoping you'd say that." He didn't like having Alexis and Denali near this guy, but they were running out of time. Maureen's abduction changed everything.

He pulled the list up on his phone. It was longer than he'd have liked, but starting with those registered to people living in or around Greybull would help.

They were back at the hotel a few minutes later. Instead of heading straight to their room, he detoured to the small business center. The computer was available, so he logged into his email. He'd already sent the list to his personal email. Doing that was against policy, but he didn't have time to waste.

When he opened the attachment, he winced when he noticed there were just over fifty trucks listed. Fifty-two to be exact. The list was in a spreadsheet format, so he took a minute to sort the file by city. There were six trucks in Greybull.

Six was doable. He requested two copies, then hit the print key. He waited impatiently for the printer to warm up and spit out the document.

"Here." He handed one copy to Alexis who stood with Denali off to the side of the small space. "Six trucks registered in Greybull."

"I see that." She frowned. "None of these names are familiar. The older guy, Gary's name isn't on the Greybull list either."

"That's okay. With only six trucks listed, we'll drive around until we find them all." He rose. "Do you need anything from the room?" He was anxious to hit the road.

"More water for Denali." Alexis turned to head toward their suite. "I'll refill the empty water bottles from the sink."

He didn't argue, knowing that giving the K9 water was part of the search routine. Alexis had mentioned how important it was to keep the dog's mucous membranes moist. Something even more crucial in these hot summer months.

Five minutes later, they were back in the SUV. He'd completely forgotten about taking ibuprofen for his knee and decided it could wait.

Maureen could not.

He scanned the six addresses and plugged them into the map app on his phone. After taking a moment to get his bearings, he chose the address closest to their current location. Interestingly, it was also the closest house to the campground where Maureen had been taken. He doubted this guy would be that stupid, but stranger things had happened. Especially since he knew this guy was spiraling out of control. "Okay, turn right on 2nd Avenue. The house we're looking for is halfway down."

She nodded and made the turn. Upon reaching the halfway point, she slowed to a stop. "Which side of the street?"

"North side." He checked the address, then eyed the house numbers. "That's it, the dark-brown two-story."

"I don't see a truck," Alexis said. "It's either in the garage, or the owner could be at work. But we can see if Denali alerts."

Going up the truck owner's driveway would technically be trespassing, but he didn't hesitate. "Go ahead. See what she does." Even as he said the words, he knew he was pushing it.

Maybe they couldn't use the search in court, but Maureen's life was at stake. As far as he was concerned, the missing teenager along with Lindsey who saw a large gray truck was more than enough of a coincidence to use exigent circumstances to do what might otherwise be considered an unlawful search.

And if Denali alerted, he wouldn't hesitate to break down the front door to search inside the house.

Alexis parked and released the hatch. He got out of the car, standing nearby to watch Denali work. He found himself holding his breath as the K9 sniffed along the end of the driveway, then made her way up to the closed garage door.

He half expected someone to come out of the front door, demanding to know what they were doing. He alternated between watching Denali and the main entrance.

Unfortunately, the dog didn't alert, even when Alexis had the dog sniff along the closed driveway door and all the way up the front walkway. Nobody came out of the house either. Or peered at them through the windows as far as he could tell.

He swallowed a groan. One down, five more to go.

Griff tried not to think about what his next step would be if Denali didn't alert on any of the vehicles here in Greybull. Sure, they could check Cody next as that town wasn't too far away, but after that?

He scanned the list. There was no feasible way they could check every single one of the fifty-two trucks scattered across the state in eight different cities.

If they didn't find something soon, he feared Maureen Kaufman would pay the price.

11

———————

Alexis tried not to feel disappointed that Denali hadn't alerted. Obviously, there were still five more trucks to check. Yet thinking of what Griff had said about the truck possibly being registered to someone else gave her pause. "What if this guy isn't living here? If he's driving a car registered to a parent or older sibling, maybe he keeps the truck someplace else."

Griff nodded slowly. "You have a point. You may want to get into the SUV, while I check the garage."

She frowned, but then realized he may need a quick escape if anyone saw him peering through windows. "Okay. Come, Denali." Using her key fob, she opened the back hatch.

As she settled behind the wheel, she watched as Griff moved around to the side of the garage not attached to the house. She started the engine and eased forward to see better.

There was a window along the side wall. Griff was over six feet tall, but he had to stretch out to look inside. Then he turned away and jogged toward her. A moment later, he slid into the passenger seat.

"The truck is inside, so I think we can safely cross this one off our list." He clipped his seat belt. "Good thinking on your part, Alexis. I'm glad we checked."

She hoped he didn't notice her blush. "Me too. What's the next destination?"

Griff consulted his phone. "Ah, we're going to head to 5th Avenue. The addresses are confusing. Main Street is really 6th Street. But then there's a 6th Avenue too."

"I'm sure most people here don't bother to use street names; they find places via landmarks." She glanced at him. "In a town this size, everyone knows everyone else, including where they live."

He nodded, still looking down at his phone. The hour was close to five in the evening, which should work to their advantage. Those working day jobs would be home by now.

She turned onto 5th Avenue. "Which house?"

"Ah, the white one near the end of the road."

The white house had a white Ram truck sitting

in the driveway. The front door of the house was open, leaving only a screen door to keep the bugs out. She parked the SUV and turned to Griff. "They're home."

"I see that." He sat for a moment, then sighed. "Okay, here's the plan. I'll walk up to the front door to talk to them. While I do that, you take Denali around the truck."

"Okay." She killed the engine and opened the back hatch. "You'll know if Denali alerts."

He nodded and slid out of the passenger side. He waited a moment for her to get Denali hyped up about the search, then strode to the front door.

"Search! Search bad guy!" She kept her voice low so it couldn't be heard by the occupants inside.

Denali lowered her head and sniffed the ground in front of the driveway. Alexis alternated between watching Griff as he spoke to an older man who came to the door and her K9 who eagerly searched for the scent. Denali didn't alert, and after a few minutes, Griff turned from the door and joined her.

"Four more to go," he murmured.

"Do they have a son?" she asked, opening the rear hatch.

"Nope, unless they were lying." Griff glanced back at the house. "I didn't hear Denali alert, though. I only said there was a missing girl and that I was talking to the neighbors in the area."

She understood he didn't want to say too much. Once they were seated, she started the car. "Where to?"

"This next one is located on 10th Avenue north. Looks like it's a couple blocks behind the grocery store."

She remembered seeing the store, it wasn't far from the Attwell Restaurant. She headed back to what the town considered Main Street and headed north. So far, their plan wasn't helping as much as she'd hoped. There was still plenty of summer daylight left, but what would they do if Denali didn't alert on any of these places? Move to another town? She didn't like the idea of leaving the place where Maureen had been abducted.

The poor teen must have been scared to death. She tried not to imagine the horror the girl was going through.

"If none of these trucks work out, we need to reconsider our strategy." She shot Griff a quick glance in time to see him frown. "Come on, Griff. You know as well as I do that Maureen doesn't have much time. We can't drive to every city on the list. We'll need to do something else to draw the killer out of hiding."

Griff remained silent, but she could tell he wasn't happy. She slowed to turn onto 10th Avenue.

"Even if we wanted to set up a sting operation,

we can't make that happen yet tonight," he finally said. "And I'm not on board with that plan anyway. Now that the killer has Maureen, he may not be interested in you."

She disagreed with that assessment, but at that moment, his phone rang.

"Flannery," he answered curtly. Then in a whisper, he added, "Green house on the left."

She nodded and pulled to a stop near the green clapboard house. It looked to be in worse repair than the other properties they'd visited, although she knew better than to make assumptions about the killer based on the outward appearance of the home. The truck wasn't in the driveway, so she put the SUV in park and waited for Griff to finish his call.

"You've landed? Great. I'm in Greybull, so you'll need to rent a car."

It took her a moment to realize he was speaking to the FBI profiler who had flown in from DC.

"I know. The state is rural, and there's a long distance between towns. That's one of the factors that's been making it difficult to find this guy. He's picked his victims from different cities. I'm wondering if he's a truck driver of some sort, making deliveries to local businesses." Griff's tone was mild, but she sensed his frustration. "Any additional information you can provide would be great."

He listened for a minute, then glanced at Alexis. "Yes, I'd like a briefing now, if that works for you. Hang on a minute, I'm working with a K9 team, so I'm going to put you on speaker."

"A K9 team from the bureau?" a female voice with a distinct East Coast accent asked.

"No, a local K9 team," Griff explained. "Alexis and her K9, Denali, found the remains of the first two missing girls, Josie and Megan. Her dog is trained to find cadavers and happened to find them while Alexis was hiking in the mountains."

She appreciated his attempt to avoid discussing her personal life. The FBI profiler didn't need to know she'd been out searching for the remains of her parents.

"I can see how that helped," Cheri said. "But why are you still working with them?"

"Because Denali has latched onto the scent of the killer, so we've been using Denali's nose to eliminate suspect vehicles." This time, he couldn't hide his frustration. Unless Cheri wasn't astute enough to notice.

There was a long pause. "That's an interesting approach."

Alexis arched a brow at Griff. The profiler didn't sound impressed.

He shrugged as if to say he couldn't care less. "Cheri Artez, meet Alexis Sullivan. Alexis, Cheri is a profiler with the FBI. I know you've had some time to look at the file while you were flying here. Any thoughts that we can use to help find this guy?"

"I did look at the file," Cheri said. "I believe we're dealing with a young white male in his early twenties, possibly up to thirties, although personally, I peg him as being on the younger side of that spectrum."

Now it was Griff who rolled his eyes, but he simply responded, "Go on."

"His victims are all young, and the fact that they work in the service industry tells me that he meets them through their employment."

Griff held her gaze, shaking his head in disappointment as if clearly hoping for more. "That may be how he identified his first three victims, but the fourth and most recent one was taken from a local campground."

"A fourth victim already?" Cheri sounded surprised.

"Yep, taken late last night, although we didn't learn about it until midday today." Griff frowned. "There must be something else triggering him, right? Don't these serials usually have mommy issues or some other type of physical or emotional abuse in their past that they're trying to take out on their victims?"

"Abuse as a child is very common," Cheri

agreed. "And I'm sure there is a triggering event, but whatever it is, it's not obvious. Maybe a scent of some sort? We should ask the families of the victims what type of perfume their loved one liked to wear. Maybe it's something that smelled like his mother."

"We can check that," Griff said. "In the meantime, we're searching the area here hoping to find him before he kills his fourth victim."

"He's escalating," Cheri said, her tone thoughtful. "The time between victims is shrinking dramatically."

Alexis sighed. This woman might be helpful in some cases, but so far the profiler hadn't told them anything they didn't already know or suspect for themselves. Except maybe a specific scent drawing him in.

"Yeah, that concerns me too." Griff's restraint was admirable, as she could see the annoyance etched on his features. "The most recent victim is Maureen Kaufman, and she's only seventeen, making her his youngest victim yet. I think she was more of a crime of opportunity, compared to the first few victims who, as you said, were likely taken because he ran into them while they were working."

"Seventeen," Cheri echoed. "That's terrible."

"Yeah. He's taken two victims from Greybull, although Maureen is technically from Cheyenne. Still, the two most recent girls were taken within a few miles of each other, which makes us believe he lives in the area. Or at least knows the town well enough to navigate the city without drawing undue attention."

"Interesting. This could be a sign he's losing control," Cheri murmured.

"I know. That's why I asked you to drive here to Greybull." Griff stared out the window for a moment. "My gut is telling me he's nearby. We're following up on some other leads that may help us pinpoint his location."

"I understand. I'll be there as soon as I can," Cheri said.

"Sounds good. I have to go, but we'll chat later." Without saying anything more, Griff punched the end-call button. He scowled and rubbed his hands over the stubble on his cheeks. "I knew she'd be useless."

"Maybe she'll be more help once she gets here." Alexis tried to be diplomatic. "If she has time to examine the victims more closely, she might find a connection between them that we've missed. The scent idea was a good one. We can certainly ask Maureen's parents what perfume she wore."

"Yeah. I'll text her parents." His thumbs flew across the phone screen, then he pocketed the phone. "We'll see if Cheri has anything else to add." He turned to look at the green clapboard house. "No sign of the truck. Let's see if Denali alerts anywhere along the driveway before I peer into the garage."

She opened the back hatch, then slid out of the car to meet Denali. "Are you ready to search?" She offered the K9 water, since she hadn't done that recently. After taking a quick drink, Denali looked up at her with steady brown eyes, clearly anticipating the job at hand. "Search bad guy!"

Her K9 went to work. But as before, Denali didn't alert anywhere on the driveway or near the garage or the front door. She called the dog back to the SUV as Griff went up to the garage to look inside. Personally, she wasn't sure the garage door even worked.

After a minute, he shook his head. "Nothing in the garage, so we may want to keep this guy on the list until we know for sure who lives here. Maybe the homeowner is a parent and drives something other than the truck. I guess we move on to the next one."

She nodded, glancing at her dog. "I agree. I feel bad, though. It's hard to keep asking Denali to search without being able to reward her. When we work disaster sites, she pretty much always finds something." She bent to scratch the dog behind the ears. "You know you're good at your job, right?"

Denali wagged her tail.

Griff sighed and glanced around. "I wish she

would alert. I'm starting to wonder if we're on the wrong track. Time is ticking by, and Maureen is still missing. I really thought the Ram truck would be our best lead."

He looked so dejected, and she knew Maureen's fate weighed heavily on his shoulders. She slipped her arm around his waist to give him a quick hug. "The truck is a good lead. I'm sure it will pan out."

He surprised her by pulling her close. "You and Denali are amazing," he whispered against her hair.

Her pulse skittered. It was hard to think when she was in his arms. "You said that already."

"I can't say it enough." He tightened his hold before releasing her. "I feel blessed to be working with you."

Then, without warning, he abruptly hauled her into his arms again and kissed her.

She melted against him, kissing him back, barely noticing a large truck pass them and pull into the driveway of the green house. Not until Griff broke off their kiss to whisper, "Can you see the driver? He's behind me."

She belatedly realized he'd kissed her as a distraction. Willing her erratic pulse to settle, she peered over his shoulder in time to see an older man slide out from the truck. "Yes. He's too old to be our guy. But we can still check him out."

Griff stepped back from their embrace and

turned casually to see for himself. "You're right about that. Give me a minute to talk to him."

She turned to Denali. "Search! Search bad guy!"

Her K9 sniffed the area but didn't alert. When Griff came back toward her, his resigned expression indicated he'd struck out. "Time to move on to the next truck."

She nodded and opened the back for Denali. She shouldn't have been hurt that he'd kissed her to make it look as if they weren't staking out the house.

But deep down, she wished Griff had kissed her for real.

GRIFF KNEW he shouldn't have kissed Alexis again. Her unique scent was imprinted in his mind, and he wanted nothing more than to kiss her again.

Especially since she'd kissed him back, sending his pulse skyrocketing. He'd even forgotten about the truck until it turned into the driveway.

Should he apologize? He glanced over, noting she didn't look upset or angry. Still, women were good at hiding their feelings.

At least, that's how Grace had been.

He momentarily looked up at the sky. If heaven was real, Grace was up there now finally at peace. Somehow, he knew Grace wouldn't mind that he'd kissed Alexis. She'd been clear from the moment they'd learned her diagnosis that she'd wanted him to move on after she was gone.

He was the one who'd resisted doing so.

"What's the next address?" Alexis asked, interrupting his thoughts. He focused on the case before them with an effort.

The moment to apologize had passed, so he let it go. He looked down at his phone. "The next address is 8th and Railroad Street."

"That's behind the Attwell Restaurant." Alexis drove there without hesitation. "I bet that's our house. There's a white Ram truck in the driveway."

"That's the one." He thought the car looked as if it had been recently washed. To remove blood stains? Maybe.

But Denali didn't alert, and all too soon they were back in the SUV.

"Two more properties to go." He consulted the map app on his phone. "Let's head to the one on Rimrock Road."

"Okay. I'll have to go back to Highway 14 to get there," Alexis said. "That's the best route to cross the river."

He nodded, scanning the traffic around them. Their search so far was disheartening, especially considering the fact that Cheri Artez's contribution hadn't provided any useful information. In his opinion, her analysis of their unknown subject wasn't worth the price of the airfare.

Not a good use of the taxpayer dollars, but he had bigger issues to worry about. They'd checked four trucks without success. And time was running out.

He needed something to go on, and soon.

They rode in silence for a few minutes. Griff straightened in his seat when he noticed the houses on the other side of the river were spaced farther apart. Something that would work in the killer's favor.

If their perp had killed the girls at his home. Griff frowned, thinking that through. Had this guy brought Josie Allen and Morgan Riley all the way across the state to kill them here?

Or had he strangled the girls in the back of his Ram truck and simply transported their bodies here?

Then again, if the guy was a trucker, he had a work vehicle that could have been used for his abductions and murders. He knew the perp used the Ram truck to tow the four-wheeler to the campground parking lot, but the actual killings may have taken place in a different vehicle.

The inconsistencies were driving him crazy. What if they were wrong about him being a trucker? Or about the Ram truck?

His thoughts whirled, and he abruptly stopped and opened his heart to prayer.

Please, Lord Jesus, grant me the wisdom to find Maureen before it's too late!

The prayer helped calm his fears. When he realized Alexis had turned onto Rimrock Road, he looked at his phone to verify the house number.

"It's the large dark-brown house set back from the road. I don't see a truck in the driveway, though." His pulse kicked up a beat. "But there is a big outbuilding. See how the driveway is formed in a Y? One branch leads to the house and garage, the other to the outbuilding. Maybe that's where he keeps the four-wheeler and trailer!"

"Or a boat." Alexis gestured to the water. "See how the back of the house is situated up against the river? The owner of this house may have a fishing boat and trailer back there."

"Spoilsport," he groused, although she had a point. It was hard to imagine a serial killer living in a nice house like this one. He just wanted something tangible to help find this guy. "We'll check it out the same way as before. You take Denali around the driveway. Since there's an outbuilding here, I'm going up to the door to see if anyone is home." What he really wanted was to look inside the outbuilding, but he knew it was likely locked. Most people didn't lock the doors to their homes out here, but something that held boats, ATVs, and other large recreational vehicles was an exception to the rule.

"Works for me." Alexis opened the back and paused, glancing at him. "I need to feed Denali dinner shortly. I gave her one of Anna's cookie bones earlier, but it's still been a long time since breakfast." She grimaced as she slid out of the car. "And I can't believe I'm saying this, but I'm getting hungry too."

"Me too. We'll take a break soon." He winced as he eyed his watch. It had taken them an hour to check the first three properties. Granted, that included the call with Cheri Artez, but still. "This shouldn't take long."

"Okay. Hey, girl, are you ready? Huh?"

Griff let Alexis and Denali do their thing. Resting his hand on the butt of his weapon, he approached the house. Up close, he noted the property had been well maintained. He knocked on the door sharply.

Nobody answered.

His pulse kicked up with anticipation. Was the killer hiding inside? He turned to watch Denali for a moment, then knocked again.

Still nothing.

He moved to the side to peer into the window. Unable to discern any movement, he turned and headed back to the driveway.

Denali sniffed intently along the edge of the garage door but hadn't alerted. He hurried to the outbuilding and tried the door.

As he feared, it was locked.

Denali trotted toward him. Still no alert. His shoulders slumped as he realized this was another dead end.

"The garage and outbuilding don't have windows," Alexis observed. "That's rather odd, isn't it?"

"Yeah, but maybe the owners don't want kids peering in to see their stuff." He managed a smile, despite feeling depressed that the Ram truck lead hadn't produced a perp. "Only one more house to check."

"I think you should keep this one on the list," Alexis said, as they got settled back in the SUV. "We haven't seen the truck, and maybe the killer had removed the SUV and trailer a while ago. He may be staying somewhere else, instead of coming back here."

"I will. Although I'm starting to worry that our guy isn't living in Greybull after all." He consulted his phone. "The next house is up off Horseshoe Lane. That's not far from here."

"I passed the road on the way here," Alexis said. "It circles around the subdivision."

When they reached Horseshoe Lane, he found the property in question. This one was the complete opposite of the previous home. The house was a double-wide trailer without a garage. The gravel driveway was rutted. It was exactly the place he'd imagined a serial killer would live, except for the fact that their perp had access to an ATV and trailer.

Not to mention a Ram truck. Even used, they weren't cheap.

"I'm staying close to you while Denali sweeps the area," he said.

"No argument here." She grimaced. "I can just imagine somebody inside with a rifle aimed at anyone who dares trespass."

He didn't like putting Alexis in danger, but skipping it wasn't an option. The owner of this double-wide had a Ram truck registered to this address. He forced himself to get out of the car. "I'll stay between you and the house."

He kept a wary eye on the front door and main window as Alexis revved up Denali to search. Then he made sure he was ahead of the pair as they went to work.

Denali didn't alert, and nobody came out of the trailer.

"Last one," he said as they once again climbed back into the SUV. "If that's not our guy, then we'll need to go back to the list of trucks to see if there's a way to narrow our search." He sighed. "Maybe I should go by age. At least for starters."

"Let's pick up a pizza on the way back to the hotel," Alexis suggested. "I'll feed Denali, then we'll examine that list of vehicles."

"I like pizza." He managed a grin despite his despair. "The works?"

"Of course!" She shot him an amused glance as she cranked the wheel into a turn. "I grew up with six brothers. I can handle—"

Her voice was cut off by the crack of gunfire. The SUV jerked, and he wondered if they'd been hit. But there wasn't any broken glass that he could see.

Alexis stomped on the gas, aiming the car toward Highway 14. He spun in his seat to see where the shot had come from.

Had someone come out of the last two properties they'd just investigated? And if so, which one?

12

———

When Alexis heard the gunshot and felt the SUV jerk in her hands, she feared the worst. That Denali may have been struck by a bullet puncturing the vehicle along the back crate area. She heard Griff calling 911 to report the shooting, but her attention was on the road and the rearview mirror.

Denali's head poked up as the dog looked around curiously. A wave of relief hit hard. Her K9 appeared to be okay.

But she knew a bullet had struck the SUV.

Concentrating on getting as far away from the shooter as possible, she quickly turned left onto Highway 14, heading in the opposite direction of Greybull. She hit the gas to increase her speed, then nearly groaned as she came up fast on a slow-moving car. She barely refrained from punching the horn. They needed to get far away from here!

"Easy." Griff put his hand on her arm.

She gripped the steering wheel so tightly that her fingers began to cramp. After what seemed like eons, the slower car turned off on a side road, clearing the way. She hit the gas, sending the SUV surging forward.

"Where are you going?" Griff asked.

Her throat felt frozen, so she simply shook her head and drove. After a few miles, and when she was sure no one had followed them, she pulled over to the side of the road. She unclenched her trembling hands and swallowed against the urge to be sick. Without a word to Griff, she opened the rear hatch, bailed from the car, and headed around to check Denali.

Then she stopped abruptly when she saw the bullet opening in the passenger door. The edges of the plastic flared out, indicating the bullet had come from the other side.

"Alexis?" Griff had slid from the car too. "What's wrong—oh. The SUV was hit."

Denali had jumped down and came over to greet her, tail wagging. She managed to swallow past the lump in her throat. "Yes. The SUV jerked, and I was worried the bullet may have struck Denali." She bent to run her fingers through the dog's fur, then she checked her legs to make sure she hadn't missed anything. "Thankfully, she looks fine."

"The bullet entered the passenger door on this side." Griff opened the door to look inside. "It went all the way through both rear passenger doors."

"If he'd hurt Denali . . ." She couldn't finish.

"I know. I'm sorry." Griff looked upset. "Did you see anyone?"

"No. One minute we were talking, the next we were being fired upon." She sighed and eyed the damaged vehicle. "I guess I should be glad it's not worse."

"I wonder if one of those two houses back there belongs to the killer." Griff stepped back to close the passenger-side door.

"Denali didn't alert." She straightened and went around to the back of the car. The crate area wasn't damaged. But the near miss made her blood boil. "Maybe he followed us to that neighborhood."

"I don't know what to think." Griff scowled. "I believe Denali would alert on his scent, but the shooting so close to the last two houses we checked bothers me. I don't believe in coincidences."

A niggle of unease had her looking at Denali.

Her K9 wasn't a tracker. She excelled at finding dead people.

"That doesn't make sense." She gave Denali the hand signal to jump in. Then she heard wailing sirens. "That must be the deputies."

"Yeah." Griff held her gaze. "We need to go back to the scene to meet with them."

She didn't want to go anywhere near the killer, but she knew he was right. Maybe the deputies could help with uncovering evidence they could use to nail this guy.

"Fine." She stepped back and closed the hatch. "You can drive. I'm not well versed in evasive driving techniques."

"You did great back there." Griff crossed over to pull her into a hug. "I'm sorry this happened. Maybe I should drop you and Denali at the hotel. I can update the local cops on what took place."

"No." She didn't want that either. "They'll need my statement. Besides, I think it's better if we stick together."

"If you're sure." He released her and rounded the SUV to slide in behind the wheel. "They won't be happy we didn't notify them about the previous shootings."

She shrugged, still feeling the effects of the jolt of adrenaline. "I was surprised you called them this time."

He glanced at her before pulling back onto the road. When the road was clear, he made a quick U-turn to drive back toward Greybull. She was beginning to despise that small town. "I wasn't sure if the vehicle was hit and, if so, how badly. If the gas tank had been hit, we may not have been able to get away."

That possibility hadn't entered her mind. She'd only cared about Denali. And Griff, too, but her K9 had been vulnerable in the back. "I should call my siblings to arrange for another vehicle."

He nodded. "Hold off until we talk to the deputies. Maybe they'll find something useful."

She took several deep breaths to calm her racing heart. The more she thought about the shooter being in the neighborhood on the other side of the river from the main part of Greybull, the more she wondered about the two addresses they'd investigated.

Could the killer have left his truck somewhere else and walked to the properties? She felt certain Denali would have alerted if this guy had gotten close to the house.

Were they missing something? Some connection that would point them to the killer?

Possibilities whirled in her mind until her head began to throb. She massaged her temples as Griff returned to the scene of the shooting. He turned off the highway back to the small neighborhood they'd left just minutes ago.

Seeing the deputy's vehicles up ahead in the road, red and blue lights flashing, made her feel a little better. Surely this guy wouldn't make another attempt against her with the cops around.

Then again, it wasn't as if Griff's presence had put him off. Quite the opposite. She had the feeling the killer would gladly take them both out of the picture.

But her most of all.

She recognized Deputy Paul Holland and Deputy Cameron Newton. "What happened?" Paul asked.

Griff stepped forward. "We have a lead on the serial killer. A witness saw him getting into a light-colored Ram truck pulling a trailer with a four-wheeler on the back. We've been scouting the addresses in Greybull that have Ram trucks registered to the owners. Two of those properties are located here in this part of town."

"No license plate number?" Cameron asked.

"Nope. The only reason we know it's a Ram is because our fifteen-year-old male witness knows his trucks." Griff gestured to the road beyond. "The first house we checked is that large brown one with the outbuilding. We thought that might be where the four-wheeler and trailer are stored. But Denali didn't alert."

Paul's gaze shifted to her. "I thought Denali was a cadaver dog?"

"She is. But somehow she's latched onto the killer's scent. Probably because she knows he's a threat to me." She glanced at Griff. "You already know he took a shot at me near the burial site of the two missing girls. He also fired at us at the hotel, was that last night?" She'd lost track of time with everything that was going on. When Griff nodded, she went on. "And now this. If you look at my SUV, you'll see where the bullet went in one rear passenger door and went all the way through and out the other side."

Cameron frowned. "Show me."

She turned and gestured to the smaller bullet hole on the passenger side. "The bullet went in here." She walked around the rear to show the deputy the other side. "You can see it obviously exited here."

"Yeah." Cameron took several pictures with his cell phone.

Paul came over to see for himself. Then he turned toward Griff. "You didn't see anyone shooting?"

"No. But I don't think our checking these addresses and being fired upon in the same location is a coincidence." Griff frowned. "I just don't understand how this guy could be using one of these properties as a home base if Denali didn't alert on either one."

"Maybe there's a hunting cabin in the vicinity," Paul suggested. He gestured toward the large brown house. "The owner there could have another property."

Alexis nodded. "We did consider the killer may be using a truck that belongs to a parent or sibling."

"I'll investigate that possibility," Griff agreed. "The other house we checked is a little farther down. It's a double-wide trailer home in rough shape. There's no garage or outbuildings, and we didn't see a truck either."

"We'll check it out," Cameron said. "But if you think this guy has access to a cabin in the woods, I think the owner of the brown house is the more likely option."

Griff consulted his phone. "The truck at that address is registered to a Calvin Jenkins. Does that ring a bell?"

Both Paul and Cameron shook their heads. "Nope," Paul said. "And we know most of the troublemakers in the area."

The name was vaguely familiar, but Alexis couldn't place it. Had there been a Jenkins in the high school in Cody? She couldn't imagine why

Calvin Jenkins's son would go all that way. This home was on the east side of Greybull. Cody was west of here. A few families on the west side of town had made the trip, but that was mostly for kids interested in playing football or basketball.

Greybull was small enough that they didn't have a lot of options for sports.

"Can Denali find shell casings?" Paul asked.

She grimaced. "We can try, but that's not her area of expertise. Many of the tracking K9s have been cross-trained to find gold, and I've tried with Denali. She's hit or miss."

"But she may find the bad guy's scent," Griff reminded her.

"True." She knelt to a crouch beside her dog. "I'll work that angle instead." She scratched Denali behind the ears. "Are you ready? Huh? Ready to search? Search bad guy!"

Denali's tail wagged, and the K9 quickly turned to sniff the ground. Alexis followed as did Griff. She scanned the area with apprehension. As much as she wanted to believe the killer was long gone, she didn't put anything past him.

Especially now.

Denali didn't follow a straight path, but veered one way, then the other. Her K9 headed north, which made sense as they'd been driving south when the SUV had been hit. She followed her K9 between two houses to the next road.

Denali picked up the pace, her nose to the ground now as if she'd caught the scent. Alexis felt her pulse spike with fear. Was the killer nearby watching their progress? Being out in the open like this made her feel vulnerable and exposed.

Griff came up beside her. "Are you okay?"

She managed a nod, even though she was far from okay. She kept her gaze on Denali as the dog turned and sniffed a specific section of the side of the road. Then she sat and let out a bark.

Alexis lunged forward to examine the area where Denali alerted. She didn't see anything at first, but then she caught a glimpse of brass that was mostly hidden in the tall grass. "Griff?" She looked over her shoulder. "She found the shell casing."

Griff quickly dropped down to see for himself. "Looks to be the same make and model as the other shell casing."

"Let me see." Paul must have been trailing them. He knelt beside Griff, then rose to his feet. "Looks like our perp was standing here with a rifle when he took the shot."

Alexis shivered as she realized there was a direct line of sight from here to the street they'd been on. If she hadn't turned at the right moment, the outcome could have been very different.

"I'm sure he was standing on the ground," Griff said. "If he'd been positioned in the truck bed for example, the bullet would have struck the SUV higher." He lifted his arms as if simulating a rifle shot. "And the bullet would have had a downward trajectory rather than hitting straight on."

"Maybe this guy isn't a hunter," Paul said with a shrug.

"Oh, he's a hunter." Griff scowled darkly. "He just chooses to hunt young women rather than elk."

Alexis shivered again. Only a very evil man would hunt and kill young women. Was Maureen already dead? She didn't know.

Thinking of that poor girl had her steeling her resolve. She squared her shoulders. They needed to set a trap for this guy.

And if that meant putting herself in harm's way, then so be it. Better that than to let him prey on more young girls.

GRIFF WATCHED as Paul bagged the shell casing. Every bit of evidence helped, but he was anxious to get back to the hotel to use the computer. If Calvin Jenkins owned a cabin nearby, he wanted to find it.

Even if that meant approaching the place at night.

"We need to get back to the hotel." Griff began walking back to where they'd left the SUV. "There's more work to do."

"Understood." Paul didn't argue. "We know how to reach you."

"I may need your help, though." Griff eyed the deputy. "If I find this guy owns a cabin, I'll want you and Cam and others to go with me."

"Absolutely." Paul frowned. "You think Maureen is still alive?"

"I hope so." Griff tried not to think the worst.

"I have a computer in the squad," Paul said. "We can check if Calvin Jenkins owns a cabin before you go."

"Great." He glanced at Alexis who stayed close to his side. "Can Denali wait a few more minutes for dinner?"

"Yes. There's food in the back of the SUV." She turned to look behind them. "It's hard to stay out here, though, knowing he could be nearby."

"I know." He longed to pull her into his arms. To reassure her he wouldn't let anything bad happen.

But that was a promise he couldn't keep. The shooter had hit their SUV without his even knowing the guy was in the area. Griff imagined the killer had parked his Ram truck, maybe watching them with binoculars as they worked. Then took the opportunity to fire at them.

Why he hadn't done that when they were walking outside in the open, he wasn't sure.

Unless the shooter had only intended for them to crash so that he could take Alexis by force.

"Hey, Cam, would you start canvassing the neighbors around the location where we found the shell casing?" Paul asked. "I'm going to let Griff log into my computer. In the meantime, having a better description of the Ram truck would help. If we knew a specific color, we could ask all deputies to stop and question the drivers."

"Sure." Cam didn't hesitate. "Join me as soon as you can."

"Will do." Paul opened his squad door and slid in behind the wheel. Then he punched the keys to the computer mounted inside. Griff waited until he was finished, then took his place.

He started with a background search on Calvin Jenkins. The guy was clean. He found the property listing for the house, then searched for additional properties owned by Jenkins.

Nothing popped up.

His heart sank. No cabin? He'd felt sure there had to be a connection. He looked for civil actions and found a marriage and divorce.

Calvin's wife's name was Elise Sanford. He searched for properties under her name but didn't find anything.

He resisted the urge to smack the steering wheel. Paul leaned in. "No luck?"

"No." He slid out of the squad. "I'm going to keep searching, though. I'll dig into the backgrounds of all the owners of the other property too. And maybe see if there are grandparents involved." Doing so would take time.

Time Maureen Kaufman didn't have.

"Okay, keep us informed," Paul said. "We're working second shift and will be on duty until eleven tonight."

"I will, thanks." He turned toward Alexis. "Ready to grab that pizza and head back to the hotel?"

She nodded, her expression troubled. "I really hoped the cabin idea would have helped narrow our search."

"It still might." He strove to sound positive. "I feel like we're getting close."

They hurried back to the SUV. Once Denali was secure in the back and they were seated, he pulled away from the curb.

"We need to set a trap for him." Alexis pinned him with a look. "If we don't find a cabin to search, that has to be our next step."

"I'm not—"

"You have to," she interrupted. "He has likely already killed Maureen, and that means other girls are at risk too. This must end, Griff. Now. Tonight."

He wanted to argue. But there was no denying time was running out. "We'll see. I think we'll find a cabin connected to one of those two homes."

"The double-wide?" She scoffed. "Doubtful."

"You never know. Maybe the killer's family moved from the double-wide to live in the cabin year-round. Or they're spending the summer there." He didn't want to give up on the possibility of finding a cabin.

It was better by far than using Alexis as bait.

He didn't see a pizza place along the way back, but vaguely remembered the pub across the street had them on the menu. "We'll stop at the pub first."

"Okay." She tucked a strand of her dark hair behind her ear. "As I was saying before the gunfire, I like my pizza with the works."

"Duly noted." He tried to smile. "We're getting close. I can feel it."

"Not close enough." She winced, then added, "Sorry, I'm just feeling depressed. It seems like every time we get one step closer, we're thrown three steps back."

"I hear you." He understood and shared her frustration. The killer may have seen them coming to the neighborhood, managing to get away in time. The way he kept taking shots at them, though, seemed reckless. Sooner or later, someone would see and identify him.

Maybe the canvass would turn up something useful. "Stay here. I'll head inside to order."

She nodded, and he thought it was a testament to her exhaustion that she didn't press to follow him inside. The place was packed, and he immediately realized they should have called in their order.

When he found a server, she confirmed his suspicion. "There's a twenty-to-thirty-minute wait. You want to come back to pick it up?"

"Do you deliver across the street?"

"Yes. Give me your room number." She took down the information, and he paid for the meal.

"I figured." Alexis sighed when he returned to the SUV to give her the news. "Summertime is busy around here."

He should have thought of that for himself. "They'll deliver it when it's ready." Griff drove across the street and went around to the back to park. He opened the back for Denali.

Alexis hauled the large pack out of the back seat. It had been on the floor, or the bullet would have hit that too. "Come, Denali."

He rested his hand on his weapon as he followed them inside. He paused at the doorway of their room. "I'm going to the business center to use the computer. Stay in the room with the door locked, okay?"

"Yes." She nodded at the dog. "I'll feed Denali

and then wait for you before taking her outside to get busy."

"Good. If the restaurant calls, let me know." He had to resist the urge to kiss her. "I'll be back soon."

She nodded, used her key to unlock the door, and pushed it open. Denali went through first. Griff considered clearing the room, but Denali would have alerted if someone was inside. Especially the killer.

Leaving Alexis and Denali in the room wasn't easy. He'd become accustomed to having her nearby. He wondered how he'd handle not seeing her once this was over.

The thought bothered him, but he shoved it aside. There was no time to think about his future. Not when Maureen's life was on the line.

He settled down at the computer and began searching for relatives of Elise Sanford. If his theory of the cabin was correct, it could be in her mother's name. Out here, property was often handed down from one generation to the next.

Ten minutes passed before he found an obituary for Elizabeth Holms. There, he saw the daughter's name of Elise Sanford. He wasn't sure why they didn't have the same last name, until he realized that Elizabeth Holms was also divorced.

But best of all, there were two grandsons mentioned in the obituary. James and Tyler Jenkins.

More searching revealed James Jenkins had died three months ago in what had been deemed a suicide. Tyler didn't have an online presence at all, which was odd. Most kids did.

He made a note of Tyler Jenkins's name and continued searching for additional properties that may have been owned by either Elise Sanford or Elizabeth Holms.

Another ten minutes passed before he found it. Elizabeth Holms had a mountain home. And when he put the address into his map app, he was surprised to see it was located about halfway between Greybull and Shell.

That had to be it! He jumped to his feet and headed through the lobby. A harried-looking teenager came in holding a pizza.

"That's mine, thanks." He pulled cash from his pocket to give him a tip. Then he hurried down the hall to the suite.

He ignored the rumbling of his stomach at the mouthwatering scent of the pizza. There wouldn't be time to eat. He needed to get to that cabin ASAP.

Silently praying that Maureen Kaufman would still be alive when he reached it.

He unlocked the door. "Alexis?"

Denali barked and ran back and forth from the bedroom to him. A chill snaked down his spine. He dropped the pizza on the table and reached for his gun. "Where is she? Where's Alexis?"

Denali whined and ran back to the bedroom. Griff cautiously entered the room, taking note of the fact that Alexis's gun and key fob were on the bedside table. Then he spotted the open window, and his heart dropped to the soles of his feet.

Alexis was gone. And he was sure Tyler Jenkins had her.

13

———————

Alexis swallowed against a knot of fear as her previous tutoring student Tyler Jenkins led her from the hotel at gunpoint. She should have been suspicious when she saw him through the window of her hotel room. Denali had been eating her dinner in the main living area while she'd gone to the bedroom to clean up. She'd noticed him doubled over, his arms wrapped around his stomach, moaning in pain and looking as if he might be sick. She'd called out to him, and he'd stumbled toward her. He'd looked so innocent that she'd lifted the window to help.

Then she froze when his gun was pointed at her face.

Tyler had demanded she come with him, or he'd shoot her now and be done. And then he'd shoot her dog. In a heartbeat, the innocence she'd remembered in the young Tyler she had known vanished.

She'd never considered any of the kids she'd tutored at school to be the killer. Kyle had crossed her mind because of his lack of emotion over losing his dog. Even Dave, who'd been super quiet and reserved. But Tyler? She hadn't realized he was capable of this. But he was that and more.

He was a monster.

He'd demanded she leave her gun and any bullets behind. She'd slowly removed the gun from her holster and dug in her jeans pocket for the key fob to the SUV. He must have assumed the key was ammo because he hadn't said anything. When she no longer had a weapon to defend herself, he'd forced her to go with him.

Praying Denali would lead Griff to find her sooner than later.

"Where are we going?" She wasn't surprised to see a somewhat battered silver Ram truck parked on the dead-end street behind the hotel. The same place he'd parked last night, based on Denali's previous alert.

"Get behind the wheel." He used the tip of his gun to indicate she should jump into the driver's seat.

She stepped on the running board to get in. Did she have enough courage to crash the truck by going off the road into a steep ravine? Doing so might be enough to get him to drop the gun, if the impact didn't kill them. Even with the added safety feature of airbags and seatbelts, the truck would likely roll.

"Tie this around your wrist and the steering wheel." Tyler pulled a rope from the truck floor and thrust it toward her.

"Can I put my seatbelt on first?"

"No."

She held his gaze for a long moment, then did as he demanded. "Why are you doing this, Tyler? I tried to help you back in high school."

"Tighter." He ignored her question.

With a sick feeling, she tightened the rope so that it was snug against her left wrist. Then she looped it around the steering wheel and awkwardly tied both ends together with her free hand.

"Good." His eyes were dark and soulless as he stared at her. "Don't try anything or you'll lose an arm at the very least."

She nodded, realizing he was right. Without the seatbelt and with her arm tied to the wheel, she couldn't try to crash. She'd have to come up with some other way to escape. How, she had no clue. "Tyler, please, why are you—"

"Shut up." He stepped back and slammed the door since she couldn't use her left wrist to do it herself.

Silently praying for strength, she sat perfectly still until Tyler climbed into the seat beside her. After connecting his seat belt, he pressed the gun into her side. "Drive slowly and carefully. You try anything, I'll shoot."

"I understand." She started the car and pulled away from the curb, feeling naked without the seat belt across her chest.

"Turn left," he directed.

Having no choice, she turned. She scanned the road ahead but didn't see any police vehicles. How long would it take for Griff to notice she was gone?

Too long.

"Is Maureen still alive?" She pushed the question through her tight throat.

"Shut up." He was calm, but she sensed he was walking on the edge. "Get on Highway 14 heading east."

East would take them out of Greybull toward the Bighorn Mountains. Had Griff found a cabin linked to one of the properties? She prayed he had and kicked herself for not remembering Tyler's last name was Jenkins.

This was all her fault for not going through the names of all her tutoring students with Griff.

She turned onto Highway 14 but didn't increase her speed because she was too busy looking at the sheriff's deputies that were still parked in the residential area on the other side of the river. As they rolled past, she willed one of the deputies to glance over and see them.

They didn't.

"Faster, but not over the speed limit." Tyler's icy voice sent a ripple of fear over her. She risked a quick glance toward him. There was not an ounce of emotion reflected on his features. He would kill her without a smidgen of remorse.

The way he'd killed Josie, Megan, Wendy, and likely Maureen.

She pushed harder on the accelerator to increase their speed. The police vehicles were well behind them now and of no help to her. The rope bit into her wrist; she wasn't used to driving basically one handed. And every turn she made twisted her left elbow and shoulder to a painful angle.

Nothing as bad as the fate that awaited her. Panic welled in her chest, and she willed it back, trying to think. She needed to stall for time. If they were headed to a cabin the way she thought they were, Griff would find them.

Hopefully in time to save her.

"In three miles turn left." Tyler's cold voice broke into her thoughts.

"Okay." She racked her brain for something to say. "Why did you stop coming to our tutoring sessions?"

He ignored her question. The gun he held pressed against her side never wavered.

Alexis had a bad feeling that he wouldn't hesitate to kill her once they'd reached their destination.

"Maureen's parents are worried about her." The words barely left her mouth when he jabbed the gun harder against her ribs.

"What part of shut up don't you understand?" The eerie calmness did not reassure her. "You can talk when I say you can talk."

Okay, so this was a control thing. Tyler needed to always maintain control over his victims. She remembered what the ME's report said about the possibility of his using drugs prior to strangling his victims.

Would he drug her too? Probably. A ripple of aversion washed over her, but she tried not to lose hope. Griff would find her.

She tried to make eye contact with the drivers of other vehicles to no avail. The speed limit was high enough that the cars whizzed past.

"Turn here." She was so engrossed in trying to communicate her situation to other drivers that she'd completely forgotten his instruction to turn left in three miles.

Without answering, she obliged by slowing down to safely make the turn onto Hawkeye Road. Here they were the only car on the road. They passed one house that she could see through the trees, but after that, there was nothing but wooded acres of land.

"Go for another four miles," Tyler said. "There's a two-track road to the right."

"Okay." Ironically, they weren't that far from Greybull. Maybe halfway between the towns of Greybull and Shell.

Griff had been right about the killer staying close. And about how his attacks against her had been more than just eliminating the chance to be found via her K9.

It had turned personal.

She didn't ask any more questions, though, for fear he'd simply shoot her. He was buckled in and would likely survive a crash.

"I should have killed your dog before we left." Tyler's voice sounded annoyed. The first emotion she'd noticed since he'd taken her away by gunpoint. He jabbed the gun against her ribs again. "If I see that dog of yours, I'll shoot him."

"I believe you." She wasn't a chatty Cathy by nature, but keeping silent was more difficult than she'd ever imagined. The need to know what was going through Tyler's mind threatened to burst free. She was desperate to understand why he'd started to stalk and kill young women.

Especially what had caught his attention about

the four very different victims. If she didn't include herself.

There was a very real possibility she'd end up dead as Tyler's fifth victim.

She drove in silence for a few minutes. The sun hadn't set, but it was far enough on the horizon that the light was muted by the trees around them. Would Griff find her before darkness fell?

She wasn't sure she would last that long.

"Turn here." Tyler's voice again breached her thoughts.

The two-track road wasn't marked in any way. If someone didn't know it was there, they'd drive right past.

She slowed and made the right-hand turn, her left arm swinging up and over the steering wheel with the movement. At least right turns didn't hurt as much as going to the left.

The Ram truck bumped along the two-track road for more than a hundred yards before the small log cabin came into view. The exterior brown logs with dark-green trim painted around the windows and doorway helped camouflage the building from view against the backdrop of the woods. In the darkness, the cabin would be even more difficult to see unless there were lights coming from inside.

There were no visible lights now. She swallowed hard, fearing he'd already killed Maureen.

"Go around to the back of the cabin and park there."

"Okay." She made the loop around the cabin and found an open area to park. She shifted into park, then sat waiting for his instructions.

Would he kill her here? Or force her to walk into the woods?

Would she eventually end up in the burial field where they'd found the other victims? They had put up the cameras, but getting Tyler on film would be too little, too late.

No, she told herself. *Not too late.* All that really mattered was for Tyler to be caught and arrested and thrown in jail for the rest of his life.

She drew a deep calming breath, lowered her chin, and silently prayed

Lord Jesus, please keep Griff, Denali, and Maureen safe in Your care. If my life is to be sacrificed for the others, then so be it. Let Thy will be done. Amen.

GRIFF CALLED Deputy Paul Holland as he led Denali to the SUV. He wasn't sure why Alexis had set her gun and key fob aside, unless she'd been planning to change clothes?

A more likely scenario was that Jenkins had told

her to leave the gun behind, and she'd subtly pulled the key fob out too.

He had no idea how the killer had gotten to her, but he felt certain he knew where she was. The cabin that was owned by Tyler Jenkins's maternal grandmother.

The title should have been switched after the old woman's death but hadn't been. Maybe an oversight as the woman had passed away earlier that year. The title wouldn't become an issue until it was time to pay property taxes.

Before Paul answered his call, a tall woman stepped in front of him. "Are you Agent Flannery?"

"Yes. I'm sorry, but I don't have time to talk." He moved to step past her, but the woman grabbed his arm.

"I'm Agent Cheri Aztec. You need to make time to talk." Her haughty tone had him grinding his teeth.

"The killer has abducted Alexis Sullivan." He wrenched free from her grasp. "I know who the killer is, so your services are no longer needed. Head inside and I'll keep you updated on the investigation."

She reared back. "You know him?"

He seriously did not have time for this. "Go." He gestured toward the hotel. "We'll talk later."

"What's going on, Griff?" Paul asked, finally answering the call.

He turned his back on Cheri. "I need you and as many other law enforcement officers you can get to meet me at the cabin." Griff opened the back hatch for Denali. She jumped in as if understanding they were heading out to find her handler. "But no lights and sirens. We'll need to meet at some point well away from the cabin to plan our approach. This guy has killed at least three women, maybe more. We can't risk him shooting and killing Alexis if we rush in."

"Understood," Paul agreed. "Text me the address."

Griff took a moment to do that, forcing himself to remain calm. Thankfully, Cheri must have taken his advice because he didn't see her. Good riddance. He wasn't as familiar with the area as the local deputies were. He'd need to let them take the lead on where to set up their rendezvous.

And he needed to stay sharply focused on the plan if he was to rescue Alexis alive and unharmed.

Please Lord? He took a moment to lift his head to the sky, opening his heart to prayer. He needed God now more than ever. And he knew in that moment he never should have turned his back on his faith after losing Grace. *Please keep Alexis safe!*

A sense of peace washed over him. He could do

this. Alexis would know he was coming, that's why she set the key fob beside the gun.

Stepping back, he closed the back hatch, then ran around to the driver's seat. His thoughts whirled as he drove to the cabin.

Was Maureen still alive? If so, they had two potential hostages. That wasn't good, yet he tried to believe the two women wouldn't just sit back and do nothing. *Especially Alexis*, he silently admitted. It would not surprise him if Alexis did something to draw Jenkins's attention away from the seventeen-year-old, even if that meant getting hurt or even killed in the process.

He and the other deputies would need to have a plan to prevent that from happening. He told himself Jenkins wasn't as smart as he thought. Using the same spot in the mountains to bury his bodies was proof of that.

At some point, Griff needed to call his boss who was no doubt getting an earful from Cheri. She'd looked annoyed to realize her services weren't needed after all.

Not that he cared, as she hadn't given them anything useful to go on in the first place.

He took Highway 14 past the intersection that led to the shooting location. He wondered how Jenkins had gotten from this location to the highway and subsequently to the hotel without them noticing.

There must be another street that crosses the river. Or the Ram had taken a wide circle around the neighborhood to get past them. The latter option was more likely, as Jenkins obviously knew the neighborhood better than they did.

If only he'd chosen to check those properties first! Maybe they'd already be on their way to the cabin, rather than giving Jenkins the opportunity to take a shot at them.

He shook off the thought. Going back and wishing he'd done things differently was a waste of time. He needed to deal with the reality that Jenkins had Alexis and might already be drugging her to kill her.

The way he had his other victims.

Denali let out a whine as he drove. He glanced at the rearview mirror to see she had her head up. The dog was perceptive enough to know Alexis was in danger.

"Soon, girl." He spoke to the dog the way Alexis would have if she was here and was surprised at how much he believed the K9 could understand his words. "We're going to find her very soon."

There was a thumping sound as her wagging tail hit the bottom of the crate in response.

If only Denali could talk, he'd know more. Then

again, he wasn't sure how it was that Denali hadn't alerted Alexis to the danger in the first place. Had they been wrong about the dog latching onto the killer's scent?

No way, Denali had proved herself over and over, tracking the suspect's scent several times, and they'd found the shell casings nearby too.

His phone rang, and he recognized Paul's name on the screen. "Take a left-hand turn off Highway 14 to Hawkeye Road. You'll find us about two miles down the road."

"I'll be there soon." Of course, the deputies had gotten there before he had. First, Cheri Aztec had held him up, and the hotel was farther away.

He increased his speed but then had to abruptly slow down as the beams of his headlights flashed on the street sign identifying Hawkeye Road. He made the turn, his headlights illuminating the cracked asphalt road.

It was surprising how quickly darkness had fallen. Forced into driving slower than he liked, he navigated the curvy road. It was after one sharp turn that he saw the two sheriff's deputy squads parked off to one side.

Only two? His heart sank. After pulling off the road behind them, he killed the engine and hit the button to open the back hatch for Denali.

If Alexis wasn't at the cabin, he prayed Denali

would be able to lead them to wherever Jenkins had taken her.

If the guy used his truck to take Alexis somewhere far away, they'd be out of luck. They'd have a better chance of finding her if the perp used his four-wheeler.

"Okay, the cabin you've identified is about two miles from here," Paul said in lieu of a greeting. "I agree that we should go in on foot, surrounding the cabin."

"Keep in mind we don't know if he has cameras posted around the property," Griff said. "I'm worried we'll tip our hand."

Paul frowned. "I'm open to suggestions."

"I don't have any." Griff raked his hand through his hair. Then his gaze landed on Denali. "I could send Denali in first, see if she raises an alarm from anyone inside." He hesitated, then added, "I'm not sure Alexis will appreciate this approach. I believe she left Denali behind on purpose to protect her K9. We already know Jenkins tried to poison the dog to eliminate her from the equation."

Paul glanced at the dog who stood beside Griff, her nose in the air as if she were already trying to find Alexis. "Alexis might not like the plan, but I do."

Griff knew if anything happened to Denali, Alexis would never speak to him again. And he wouldn't blame her. But he'd rather have her alive and angry with him than dead. He looked back at Paul. "We need to get closer to the cabin. Denali can't follow a scent trail from this far back, not if the killer drove here with Alexis in the truck."

"Understood." Paul gestured to Cameron. "Let's drive a little closer so we only have to walk a mile or so."

"Keep your headlights off," Griff advised. "It's getting dark, and the headlights can be seen from a distance. This road doesn't appear to get much traffic. Three vehicles will be too noticeable."

"Agree." Paul nodded toward Cam. "Ready?"

"I'm in," Cam agreed.

Griff went back to the SUV. The back hatch was still open, so he patted the floor of the crate. "Get in, girl."

Denali didn't move. She didn't want to get in.

He tried again. "Up, Denali. Up. I promise we're going to find her."

Denali looked to where the deputies had pulled back out into the road. Even without the headlights, it was easy to see them. Griff hoped the taillights and running lights wouldn't give them away.

"Up!" He patted the crate area.

Denali gathered herself and jumped up. Grateful, he closed the hatch and quickly slid in behind the wheel to follow the deputies.

When the deputies pulled over to the side of the road, Griff did the same. He released the hatch. By the time he pushed open his driver's side door, Denali was already there, waiting.

The K9 was raring to go.

"There's a two-track road to the right less than a mile up ahead," Paul said when he'd crossed over to join them. "I think you should take Denali about three-quarters of the way, then cut into the woods. The more cover, the better."

"Sounds good." Dropping to one knee, he put his arm around the dog. "I need you to find Alexis, but you also have to promise to be careful. Don't get hurt, okay?"

Denali stared up at him. He wanted to believe the dog understood but knew that was impossible. Still, he gave the dog a hug, hoping and praying this would turn out all right.

That he wouldn't put Denali in danger for nothing.

He rose and went back to the SUV. The hatch was still open, and he rummaged around until he found water and a collapsible bowl. Thankfully, the Sullivans packed for every contingency.

After pouring some water in a bowl, he offered it to Denali. The dog lapped at it, then looked up at him again.

"Search bad guy." He hoped the dog would

follow his command. From what he'd learned since meeting the Sullivan siblings, each dog generally only listened to their specific handler. The K9s might be cross-trained in different search objectives, but they weren't cross-trained to listen to others.

In this case, he didn't have to worry. Denali wheeled around and trotted down the road. It was interesting that the K9's nose was in the air, not sniffing along the ground.

Griff quickened his pace. The two deputies stayed back, giving the dog room to work.

He slowed when he realized the two-track was only a few feet ahead. He'd come closer than he'd intended, but that was okay. He'd backtrack a bit once they got into the woods.

"Denali," he whispered. The K9 turned her head to look at him. "This way." He tried to mimic the hand signal Alexis used to get the K9 to come.

He walked into the woods, keeping his gaze on Denali. "This way," he repeated softly.

To his surprise, the dog turned and followed.

The darkness and foliage forced him to walk slower. He didn't want to use his arms to move tree branches. Using the same cautious approach he used when hunting elk, he moved through the woods as stealthily as possible.

Denali did the same, her nose up in the air.

Could she capture the remnants of Alexis's scent in the air? That seemed like asking a lot.

Then again, Denali had amazed him before.

They walked for what seemed like forever before he caught a glimpse of a dark structure. He stopped and stood near a tall tree truck, peering through the darkness.

It was a cabin that blended incredibly well with the surrounding trees. He watched for a long moment but didn't see any movement.

No lights either. Or a truck.

His heart sank. Were they too late? Was Alexis already dead?

14

––––––

When Tyler roughly shoved her into the cabin at gunpoint, Alexis was surprised to see the glow of a lamp on inside. She frowned in confusion. A quick glance at the windows made her realize they were blackened out in some way. As she crossed the small kitchen area, she could see that black plastic covered every single window, blocking the ability to see any of the wooded landscape surrounding them.

Her heart sank. This must be where he brought his recent victims to kill them. And even worse, there would be no way to know when Griff arrived. If he and the deputies had figured out where she was.

She was completely on her own with a sick, deranged man who enjoyed hurting women.

A shiver of fear rippled over her, but she did her best not to show weakness. Tyler was mentally unbalanced. There was no telling what would set him off.

A low moan caught her attention. Someone else was here! Maureen? She turned to see an open doorway leading to what she presumed was a bedroom. She instinctively moved that way, but a sharp command stopped her.

"Stop! Stay where you are. Sit on the sofa," Tyler said. "I didn't give you permission to go anywhere."

Permission? He almost sounded like an overly controlling parent. Remembering what the FBI profiler had mentioned, she grimly realized Tyler fit the profile as predicted. Including the part where he had likely been abused by his mother when he was younger.

Was he echoing the orders she'd given him as a child? Was he killing his mother over and over again when he strangled a young girl to death? And if so, why the sexual assault? Had he been sexually assaulted by his mother as well?

The very idea made her feel sick. Especially as she had never realized Tyler was being abused. She didn't remember seeing any bruises or obvious signs of physical harm during their tutoring sessions. Granted, he'd been a shy child who was severely behind on his education. When she'd asked him about school, he'd muttered that he'd missed a lot of classes due to being sick. She hadn't pressed for more, but she should have. Especially when she discovered that despite being in eighth grade, he read at a fourth-grade level.

Now she understood his knowledge gap was due to his tumultuous upbringing.

"Sit down," he repeated, interrupting her thoughts. "I won't tell you again."

Moving slowly, she turned and lowered herself onto the sofa. She made sure to keep her hands where he could see them. "If Maureen is sick, I can help."

"Shut. Up." He overemphasized each word. "You are not to speak unless I ask you a question. Understood?"

"Yes." She used her voice rather than nodding. If that was Maureen in the other room, or yet another of his victims, she hoped the girl would hear them and realize she wasn't alone. "I understand."

Tyler raised the gun so that the barrel was pointing at her face. Swallowing hard, she held his gaze. Was this it? Would he just shoot her now and be done with it?

Lord Jesus, please protect me and the woman in the other room. If You choose to bring me home to You, so be it. Let Thy will be done, Amen.

The prayer helped her remain calm. She did not

fear death, but she had regrets. She wished she'd told Griff how much she cared about him.

How she'd fallen in love with him.

But maybe it was better this way. If she died in this cabin, she wanted Griff to find a woman to love. Someone to build a life with.

To have a family with.

Ironically, now that she faced her own mortality, she realized just how much she wanted that too. She would miss Griff, Denali, and her brothers and sisters.

But it seemed as if God had other plans.

As she watched Tyler staring at her with his cold, dead eyes, she decided that if she had to die today, she'd take him down with her. To do everything possible to save the woman who was in the other room.

No matter how this night ended, she would not allow this man to kill another young woman.

A renewed strength coursed through her. She could do this.

She slowly dropped her gaze. Antagonizing Tyler may not be the best approach. She needed him to drop his guard. To give her an opening that she could use against him.

What that looked like, she had no clue. Especially since he wouldn't let her talk. She'd wanted to remind him of their tutoring sessions. To see her as someone he could trust.

Yet she sensed he was too far gone for that.

The seconds stretched to a full minute. Beneath her lashes, she breathed a sigh of relief when Tyler lowered the gun to his side. It was the first time since he'd abducted her from the hotel that his weapon wasn't pointed at her or pressing into her ribs. Yet he was still too far away to make a run at him.

Patience was a virtue. The longer she could hold him off, the sooner Griff and the others would get there.

Another moan came from the bedroom. She lifted her head just enough to see Tyler glance that way. Her stomach churned at the thought of him heading inside to assault Maureen.

Would he keep the gun? Hold it on the girl? Alexis wasn't sure, but if he entered that bedroom, she'd go after him.

As if reading her mind, Tyler moved backward a few steps to open a kitchen drawer. He pulled a length of rope and came toward her. "Stand up. I want you to sit in that kitchen chair." He used the tip of his gun to indicate the hardback wooden chair.

She didn't want to obey his command, but she didn't see a way out. Rising to her feet and willing her shaky knees not to collapse, she took three steps toward the chair.

Another moan from the other room, louder this time. Again, Tyler's gaze darted in that direction.

Taking advantage of the brief distraction, Alexis threw herself at Tyler. He tried to bring the gun around to shoot her but was a second too late. The sharp report of gunfire was so close it made her ears ring as her body slammed into him, sending him stumbling backward.

They landed on the floor in a tangle of limbs. She'd hoped he'd drop the gun, but he didn't. Stretching out, she tried to grab it from him.

It was no use. He wasn't as muscular as Griff, but anger made him stronger than he looked.

Tyler grunted and shoved at her to get her off him. She did her best to hang on. Then he slammed the gun into her temple. Fierce pain ricocheted through her head. Her vision clouded, and she feared the worst.

"You're going to die," Tyler threatened.

She blinked, trying to see past the pain, knowing he was right. Her efforts to take him down with her hadn't worked. Her death would be for nothing. Once he'd eliminated her, he'd turn his attention to the girl in the other room.

The sound of a dog barking from outside the

cabin had Tyler shoving her aside and scrambling to his feet. He cursed and kicked her in the ribs. Another wave of pain exploded in her chest, and she instinctively curled into a ball to protect herself. She closed her eyes, waiting for the bullet that would end her life.

Instead, she heard the thudding sound of footsteps. Confused, she rolled over, wincing at the pain, to see Tyler disappearing from the room.

No! He was getting away!

Alexis pushed herself to her feet, her ribs screaming in protest. Then the door to the cabin burst open. Griff and Denali rushed in, followed by Paul.

"Alexis! Are you okay?" Griff grasped her shoulders, his gaze raking over her. "Are you hit?"

"No, but you need to hurry." She gestured to the bedroom. "He went that way. He's dressed in a black T-shirt and black jeans. Please, don't let him escape."

Griff glanced over at Paul, then darted into the next room. She heard him gasp, then say, "Call 911 and get an ambulance here ASAP."

"I don't have my phone." Alexis watched with a keen frustration at her inability to help as Paul used his phone to make the call as he followed Griff. Denali rubbed against her, licking her fingers. Seeing her K9 partner filled her with relief. She wanted nothing more than to lower herself to the floor and wrap her arms around the dog.

Instead, she forced herself to stay on her feet. The woman in the other room needed medical attention. Alexis managed to cross the room, the pounding in her head making it difficult to see.

Or maybe that was because of the blackened windows. It was a little like being stuck in a cave.

"He's getting away!" Griff shouted. "Hurry!"

The rumble of an engine reminded her of the four-wheeler Tyler had used to transport his victims. She fumbled on the wall for a light switch, then had to shield her eyes against the abrupt brightness.

"Help me," a feeble voice croaked.

"I'm here. You're safe." Alexis squinted at the girl on the bed. Recognizing Maureen, she gave a prayer of thanks. God had guided her here in time.

The teenager was still alive.

"You're safe," she repeated as Denali followed her into the room. A cool breeze hit her face, and she belatedly realized the window was open. That must have been what Tyler used as an escape route. She focused on Maureen with an effort. "The FBI and sheriff deputies are outside trying to find Tyler."

"Is that his name?" Maureen asked. "It sounds so normal."

Alexis rested her hand on the girl's shoulder. "I'm sorry, but he's not normal. He's very sick and has killed other girls."

"Other girls?" Maureen's eyes widened in horror. "Really?"

"I'm afraid so." She tried to smile. "But you're safe now. He won't touch you again."

"Thank you." Maureen's expression crumpled as reaction set in. "I want my mom," she sobbed.

"I know you do." Alexis sat on the edge of the bed and focused on removing the strips of fabric that had been used to tie her to the bed. Denali pushed her nose into Alexis as if to say, *I'm here if you need me.* When she finished untying Maureen, she stroked her dog's fur. Then she looked at the girl. "Can you tell me your name?"

"Maureen Kaufman. I—he found me at the Greybull campsite." With her free hand, Maureen rubbed at her temple. "He acted nice, commenting on how he'd smelled my cinnamon roll. I was going to offer him some, but he suddenly grabbed me and dragged me toward him. Before I could scream, he shoved a gun into my side and told me he'd shoot if I made a sound." She shivered. "I believed him."

Alexis remembered the crushed cinnamon roll near the campfire. In the recesses of her brain, she vaguely remembered Tyler mentioning a bakery during their tutoring sessions. Was something so simple as a cinnamon roll the reason he'd abducted Maureen?

"My head hurts, and my mouth is cottony." Maureen rubbed at her wrists. "I—I think he drugged me."

"You're probably right," Alexis agreed. "We suspect he drugged his other victims too. I also heard you moaning as you regained consciousness from whatever drug he'd given you."

"How many others?" Maureen asked.

She hesitated. "We don't know for sure. Don't worry about that now. You're safe, and that's all that matters. There's water in the kitchen. Can you stand? Are you able to walk?" With her cracked or broken ribs and pounding headache, she could barely walk herself, much less carry the girl.

"I'll try."

"Good." She stood and backed away as Maureen pushed herself upright, then swung her legs out of the bed. The teenager swayed for a moment.

"Dizzy," Maureen murmured. Then she looked up at Alexis. "How long have I been here?"

"I believe you've been here about twenty hours or so. We've been searching for you since early afternoon." She patted Maureen's arm. "Take it slow, okay? I'm sure the drugs he gave you are still in your system. Try to stand when you're ready."

Denali pressed her snout into the teenager's lap,

as if knowing the girl needed support. Maureen looked surprised, then lifted a hand to pet the dog. "So soft. How did he get here? Is he your dog?"

"Yes, but she's a female. Her name is Denali, like the national park." Alexis had to smile at how Maureen looked enthralled with her K9.

"Sweet girl," Maureen crooned. Then with determination etched on her features, she pushed herself up to a standing position.

"Easy." Alexis put a hand on her arm. "Slow and steady."

They made their way out of the bedroom. Denali stayed close to Alexis's side, as if understanding how close she'd come to being killed. The kitchen chair Tyler had intended to tie her to was lying on its side. Alexis didn't remember knocking it over but knew she must have kicked it.

A low groan escaped from her throat when she bent to pick it up. Her chest was on fire, and she hoped the cracked ribs didn't puncture a vital organ.

"Are you hurt?" Maureen asked.

"A little." She moved to the sink to fill a glass with water. "Take it slow," she advised. "You don't want to throw up."

"Okay." Maureen sipped the water. She looked as if she wanted to ask more questions, but Denali turned to stare at the door seconds before Griff walked in.

"He's gone." Griff shook his head. "I'm not sure how he got past Cam, but he used the four-wheeler to escape."

Battling despair, Alexis sank into the other kitchen chair. Denali pushed her nose into her lap as she blinked back tears. She was glad they'd saved Maureen.

But if they didn't find Tyler soon, it was only a matter of time before he abducted a young woman and killed again.

GRIFF HATED KNOWING Tyler had gotten away, yet he couldn't deny being grateful to have Alexis safe and sound. "Hey, don't worry." He knelt beside her and Denali. "We're going to find him."

She closed her eyes, rubbing her temples. He frowned at the grooves of pain bracketing her mouth.

"What happened?" He reached for her hand. "Where does it hurt?"

"Ribs and head." She grimaced. "I rushed him, and we hit the floor. That's when the gun went off. He struck me in the head, then kicked me before bolting out of here."

A red wave of anger hit hard, but he forced it back. "We need to get you both to the hospital."

"Maureen, yes." Alexis stroked Denali with her free hand. "Not me. We need to find him. Denali will track his scent for us."

"She can do that?" Maureen asked in awe. "Find people?"

"Yes." Alexis smiled. "She's very talented."

"You're hurt," Griff protested. "You need to be seen by a medical professional. I'll take Denali. She'll follow his scent for me."

"Is that how you found the cabin?" Alexis asked.

"Sort of. We followed the trail of the property ownership and narrowed in on Tyler Jenkins. From there, Denali did the rest." He squeezed her hand, then stood. "You stay with Maureen. We'll head out to find Tyler."

"I'm coming with you." Alexis pushed to her feet, a steely determination etched on her features. "Let's go. He already has a head start."

Since that was true, he didn't want to waste time arguing. The door opened, and Paul stuck his head in. "Ready?"

"Yes." He gestured to Maureen. "Ask Cam to stay here with her until our backup and ambulance arrives."

Cam, who had been standing behind Paul, pushed into the room. "This is my punishment for letting him get past me."

"No, Cam, that's not it," he assured the deputy.

"We did our best. When Maureen is safe, you can meet up with us."

"Come, Denali." Alexis took a moment to fill a shallow dish with water, offering it to her K9. Denali lapped at the water, then stared up at Alexis. She gestured to the door. "Let's go outside, okay? I don't want her to alert in here."

Griff nodded, and they headed out to the back of the cabin. Paul followed, letting the two of them take the lead. He heard the faintest sound of an engine, but then it stopped. How far had Jenkins gotten? He didn't know, but they had to try. When they were in the general vicinity of where he suspected Jenkins had kept the four-wheeler, he stopped.

Alexis looked at Denali. "Are you ready to work? Search! Search bad guy."

Denali instantly lowered her nose to the ground, sniffing the area. It did not take long for the K9 to pick up Jenkins's scent. When she did, the dog increased her pace, trotting deeper into the woods.

"I wish we knew how much gas he has in the tank," Alexis said as they hurried to keep up with Denali.

"I agree. He could be miles away by now," Paul said.

Griff tried to hide his disappointment. "Who knows, maybe he'll find a place to lie low for a while."

Alexis grimaced, either from his lame suggestion or her injuries.

Denali leaped over a fallen log. Griff followed, then stopped to give Alexis a hand. She smiled weakly in gratitude. Paul quickly joined them.

"I want you to head back if the pain gets too bad," Griff said, keeping his voice low in case Jenkins was within earshot. When she scowled, he added, "Please, Alexis. I know Denali will lead the way."

"I won't slow you down." Alexis picked up her pace.

Griff exchanged a look with Paul but didn't say anything more. Alexis would push herself to keep going until her body failed her. If that happened, he'd ask Paul to stay back with her while he continued following the trail.

More deputies should be arriving on scene soon. Time had passed with excruciating slowness as he, Paul, and Cam had gotten around the cabin to find the Ram truck, but he knew that it hadn't taken as long as he'd feared.

Still, they needed to find Jenkins. Before he killed again.

Griff lifted his heart in prayer, asking God to guide them on the right path. Denali was a superstar, moving through the woods with ease and determination. The K9 never wavered from her path.

By unspoken agreement, they fell silent as they continued through the woods. After about twenty minutes, Alexis whispered, "Griff? We'll need to give Denali a break soon."

"I understand." He didn't want to push the dog past her limit. Speaking softly, he continued, "Maybe we should give up and head back to the cabin."

"Not yet." Alexis looked from him to Paul. "I don't hear a four-wheeler, so we'll either come across a road or he's hiding someplace."

Denali abruptly stopped, sniffing one specific spot for a long moment before turning to glance up at Alexis. When Alexis put her finger to her lips, Denali simply sat there looking at her.

Griff was impressed and bent to examine the ground. Denali had jumped over a log or two, which had to be a shortcut as the four-wheeler wouldn't have been able to do that. He remembered that dogs could track skin cells that were left behind along with beads of sweat. He didn't dare use his phone but studied the ground from different angles.

There. He could make out the barest hint of tire tracks.

Denali had come through. They were on Jenkins's trail.

Alexis lowered herself to the ground, drawing Denali down too. "Rest, girl," she whispered.

Denali stretched out beside her and lowered her head between her paws, clearly familiar with the routine.

Paul stood beside Griff. "I don't like feeling exposed," he whispered. "We can barely see six inches in front of our faces."

"I don't either." Sweeping his gaze over the area, he tried not to imagine Jenkins sitting out there, waiting for them. "I'm sure he's far from here, but we need to try."

"Okay." Paul didn't look thrilled.

Alexis waited a full five minutes before struggling to her feet. In a low whisper, she said, "Search, Denali. Search bad guy."

Denali followed the softly spoken command, putting her nose to the ground and moving forward through the woods. Griff made sure he was between Denali and Alexis, leaving Paul to cover their back. And to help Alexis if she succumbed to her injuries.

They walked another ten minutes in silence before Denali abruptly veered to the left. The darkness made it difficult to see, but he believed the path was wide enough for a four-wheeler.

The K9 took them up a gradual incline. He tensed, trying to see if Jenkins was up ahead, waiting for them. He pulled his weapon, holding it down at his side, and hoped Paul had done the same.

Better to be ready for the worst-case scenario.

Denali seemed to be on a mission. She pushed forward as if eager to find the bad guy. Griff knew the Sullivan K9s viewed the search as a game, but in this instance, he was convinced the dog understood this search to be different.

There was a break in the trees allowing moonlight to stream through. Catching a glimpse of a large rock, he stopped.

Alexis seemed to read his mind. "Denali, stop. Heel."

The words hung in the air for a second. Then a crack of gunfire rang out. Griff dropped to the ground, turning to cover Alexis with his body. It took a moment for Denali to wheel around to join them. He eased to the side so that Alexis could draw her K9 close.

They'd found Jenkins.

Unfortunately, the killer had the advantage over them. Perched on higher ground, Jenkins could see them better than they could see him. Even worse, the guy had a handgun and probably a rifle, too.

It was only a matter of time before he fired again.

15

———

Covering Denali with her body, Alexis braced for more gunfire. Her pulse had jumped into the triple digits, and her breathing went shallow. Between her pounding headache and her screaming ribs, she wanted nothing more than to turn around and crawl back to the cabin.

But that wasn't an option.

She tried to take a deep breath, ignoring the fiery pain that lanced through her. Tyler had them pinned down. How well could he see them in the darkness? She wasn't sure and was afraid to move to find out.

"Paul," Griff whispered. The deputy was on her left, Griff to her right. They spoke in hushed tones over her head. "We need to split up and box him in."

"Okay," Paul agreed.

"Wait." She grasped Griff's arm to keep him from moving. Keeping her voice low, she asked, "You're going up the incline?"

"You have a better idea?" Griff's mouth was near her ear. "He has at least two weapons and who knows how much ammo."

Wincing, she knew he was right. What choice did they have? Griff and Paul heading up the mountain would leave her and Denali vulnerable. It was a better alternative than leaving the area, allowing Tyler the opportunity to escape.

No, that wasn't an option. Tyler would kill again. He was sick, partially through no fault of his own if his mother really had abused him. Yet every abused child didn't turn into a serial killer.

Besides, was her staying here any different than her original plan to use herself as bait? Nope.

"Okay," she whispered. "I'll draw his attention so you and Paul can move."

Griff frowned but must have realized there wasn't another option. "Use a rock, tossing it behind you while keeping your head down."

"Okay." She steeled her resolve to do her best. It would be easier if she didn't have Denali at her side. She worried the white areas of the dog's coat would be too easily seen. Tyler had made it clear he wouldn't hesitate to kill her K9.

The ground beneath her fingers was dry. But there was some loose dirt. Digging her fingernails into the earth provided enough dust to help hide the white fur.

Griff must have been feeling along the ground, too, because he pressed a rock into her palm. "Here. When you toss it, we'll make our move."

Curling her fingers around the rock, she nodded. Then remembering how Tyler had ordered her to shut up, she whispered, "He has control issues. I'm going to start talking to him. He won't like it, but you need to use that as your opportunity to move."

"Be careful." Griff stared down at her for a moment, then surprised her by giving her a quick kiss. Then he inched farther to the right to get ready to move. Paul mirrored his actions, inching slightly to the left.

She drew a breath, and shouted, "Tyler, it's over! Give yourself up!" Griff and Paul moved as she spoke. On the last word, she tossed the rock over her shoulder. It hit the ground with a dull thud. She quickly bent over Denali and smeared more dirt over the K9's coat.

The responding gunfire was instantaneous. She flinched, but the shot went over her head in the same trajectory as the rock.

Her heart hammered against her sternum, but she forced herself to stay put. It wasn't easy. Feeling around in the earth, her fingers closed on another rock. It was smaller, though. She wasn't sure it would draw Tyler's attention.

But she had to try.

"The cops are going to find you," she called. "It's only a matter of time." Again, she tossed the rock over her shoulder.

Tyler fired again, but this time, the bullet hit the ground just three feet away from her location. She froze, her throat tightening with fear.

Could he see her? Or was he aiming at the sound of her voice?

Likely the latter, as the rock she'd tossed had barely made a sound. Digging in the dirt, she didn't find any more rocks to use either. There was plenty of debris, though, and she slowly finished smearing bits of dirt, grass, and leaves into the white patches on Denali's coat. She relaxed a bit when she noticed the dog was much harder to see now as a result of her efforts.

How much time would Griff and Paul need to get into position?

With deliberate slowness, she scooted backward toward the base of a tree. If she could use it as cover, she could keep Tyler occupied a while longer.

She hoped.

Her fingers stumbled over a stick. It was too light to make a sound hitting the dirt, but maybe she could toss it high enough to make the leaves flutter. A long shot, but she was running out of options.

"Tyler!" She shouted his name at the top of her lungs. "Stop this right now! You're a very naughty boy!" On the last word, she threw the stick up into the tree branches, then quickly pulled Denali behind the wide trunk.

This time there was a momentary hesitation before she heard the resounding crack of gunfire. The slight pause in his reaction made her wonder if he'd momentarily imagined it was his mother yelling at him.

If so, she'd gladly play that role as long as possible.

Sweeping her hands along the ground, she searched for more rocks and sticks but found nothing.

She closed her eyes in despair. She couldn't fail Griff and Paul. She just couldn't!

Swallowing against the pain, she stretched out on her stomach, reaching her arms wide. This time, she found another rock. A bigger one than before. She drew it close, then rolled to her back. Denali licked her cheek.

"Stay," she whispered. Then she forced herself into a sitting position. She had to wait for the pain to recede before she could call out to Tyler again.

"You better listen to me, Tyler," she shouted. "You know what happens when Mommy gets mad!"

She threw the rock with all her strength, which honestly wasn't saying much. Again, there was a brief pause before the responding gunfire. She almost screamed, though, when the bullet hit the tree she and Denali were using for cover.

Not good. She pressed her back against the rough bark, her heart pounding so hard she feared it would jump out of her chest.

Maybe her attempt to camouflage Denali hadn't worked as she'd hoped. Or Tyler was getting better at pinpointing the sound of her voice. Either way, she wasn't sure how much longer she could keep him preoccupied.

Staring up at the stars she could see beyond the canopy of tree limbs, she begged for God to keep them safe.

For a long minute, she didn't hear anything. How far up the incline had Griff and Paul gotten? Close enough to see Tyler? Would they be able to take him down?

Alexis had never felt more helpless. If Griff or Paul died there tonight, she'd never forgive herself.

As if on cue, another crack of gunfire rang out. She turned to look around the tree trunk, scanning the rocky ledge above. Who'd taken the shot? Griff? Paul?

Or had Tyler noticed them coming and taken one of them out?

Alexis crawled over the ground, following the path Griff had taken. Denali came alongside, her darkened coat blending in with the foliage around them. Alexis couldn't bear the thought of either man being killed, but Griff's face flashed in her mind. *Not Griff*, she silently begged. *Please, not Griff!*

Why hadn't she told him how much she loved him when she had the chance?

Now it might be too late.

Denali stayed beside her, even though the K9 could have gotten up the incline faster. Her partner was accustomed to gunfire, but Alexis knew Denali understood the danger.

She hadn't gotten very far when another report of gunfire rang out. She instinctively ducked, drawing Denali down too.

Silence stretched for a long moment. Then she heard Griff say, "Jenkins is down, repeat, Jenkins is down. I have him in cuffs."

Relief washed over her. She lifted her gaze to the starry sky. "Thank You, Lord Jesus," she whispered.

It was over. Tyler Jenkins would never hurt anyone ever again.

～

GRIFF TIGHTENED the flexicuffs around Tyler's wrists. The young man was face down on the ground, blood seeping from the wound in his arm. Griff kicked both weapons, the handgun and the rifle, out of reach.

"Alexis? Are you okay?" It had bothered him how often Tyler had shot in her direction.

"Yes, Denali and I are fine." Her voice was strong and steady. "You're not hurt?"

"I'm not hurt." But Paul was too quiet for his peace of mind. "Paul? Are you okay?"

A low groan was his answer. Not good. He couldn't leave Jenkins to check the deputy. He didn't trust that the kid wouldn't make a run for it.

"Alexis, can you get to Paul?" He couldn't hide the sense of urgency. "I need to get Tyler down the incline."

"Yes." Griff caught movement below. He could barely make out the two forms of Alexis and Denali making their way to the other side of the incline. "We'll take a look."

Upset at the possibility of losing Paul, Griff yanked Jenkins to his feet. To his surprise, the kid didn't scream out in pain. He simply stood there, his gaze focused on something in the air over Griff's shoulder.

The young man's ability to handle pain bothered him. Obviously, Cheri Aztec had been correct in her assessment that the killer had been abused as a child. The eerily calm expression on the young man's face didn't give any insight into his thoughts.

Griff almost sympathized with the kid. Until he remembered the pale waxen expressions on his three victims' faces. Jenkins had brutally murdered them. And he would have continued his killing spree if they hadn't found him.

Another groan reached his ears. Griff pulled Jenkins toward the other side of the mountainside. It took a moment to find Paul. He'd rolled onto his side, holding his stomach as he struggled to sit up.

"Hang tough, Paul. You're going to be okay." Griff couldn't tell how badly the deputy was wounded, but the fact that he was trying to get up was a good sign. "We're going to get you back to the cabin a soon as possible."

Paul lifted his head, his features etched with pain. "Hurry," he gasped.

"I'm here." Alexis sounded breathless as she climbed the last few feet to reach Paul. She knelt at the deputy's side. Her stiff movements told Griff she was in pain too. They needed help and fast. He pulled out his phone and peered at the screen.

No service.

They'd have to get back to the cabin on their own.

Griff briefly considered tying Jenkins to a tree so

he could help Paul but decided against it. He couldn't bring himself to let the killer out of his sight.

Then he remembered the four-wheeler. He stepped in front of Jenkins. "Where's the ATV?"

Jenkins ignored him, still staring blankly over Griff's shoulder. Swallowing against a wave of frustration, Griff turned to scan the area. The darkness made it difficult to see, but he felt certain the four-wheeler wasn't far. There hadn't been that much time for Jenkins to hide it and get into position to set up his ambush.

He pulled Jenkins along as he headed toward a thick area of brush. Jenkins stumbled. Griff tightened his grip. "Don't even think about it," he warned. "I'll shoot you again if I have to."

Jenkins remained silent, still not looking at Griff. The kid was giving him the creeps.

When he reached the thicket, Griff kicked at the brush, grinning with satisfaction when his boot struck something hard. Keeping one hand on Jenkins, he moved the branches away with the other.

And found it.

"Alexis? I have the four-wheeler here." He glanced over his shoulder to where she was crouched over Paul. "We can use this to get Paul back to the cabin."

"Okay." She looked relieved. "Did you hear that, Paul? We're going to get you out of here."

Griff leaned over the four-wheeler and checked to make sure the key was in the ignition. It was. But there was no way he'd be able to drive it over to Paul while holding on to Jenkins.

"Alexis? I need you to help get the ATV over to Paul."

"Coming," she answered. "Hang on, Paul. I'll be right back."

Griff knew the Sullivans had four-wheelers and snow machines at the ranch. Alexis was more than capable of using it, but it still took some maneuvering to free the machine out of the bush.

As she drove to where Paul waited, Griff pulled Jenkins along to join them. The four-wheeler wasn't big enough for all of them to fit.

"Come on, Paul." Alexis tried to help the deputy stand. "You need to get on the back."

"Get on the ground," he told Tyler. The kid didn't obey, so he ruthlessly shoved him down. Then he leaned over to grab Paul beneath the arms, lifting him up to his feet. Once he had the deputy standing, he turned his body and set him on the back of the four-wheeler.

"Griff!" Alexis shouted in horror as Tyler staggered to his feet and ran the rest of the way up the incline.

Griff quickly followed. He didn't think the kid would get far with his wrists cuffed behind his back.

Jenkins reached the top of the incline, then flung himself forward.

"No!" Griff surged forward, trying to snag the kid's arm. But he was a split second too late. Griff stared in horror as Tyler Jenkins fell headfirst down the steep ravine. With his arms cuffed behind his back, the kid couldn't break his fall.

And when he landed headfirst, his neck clearly broken, as the rest of his body was at a ninety-degree angle, Griff knew it was too late.

Tyler Jenkins had chosen death over being incarcerated for the rest of his life.

"Oh no," Alexis breathed, coming up to stand beside him. "I can't believe he did that."

Griff shook his head and sighed. "Yeah, I did not see that one coming." He turned away, knowing there wasn't anything more he could do. There would be time to retrieve Jenkins's body later. "Let's get Paul back to the cabin."

Alexis drove while Griff sat on the back holding on to Paul who'd passed out. Denali trotted alongside. It was a slow descent, but when they reached the bottom, they found Cameron and another deputy heading toward them.

"Paul's hit." Alexis gestured to the back of the

ATV. "Griff has him, but we need that ambulance ASAP."

"I'll go." The deputy he didn't know turned and ran off.

"Where's Jenkins?" Cam asked, jogging on the opposite side of the ATV.

"Dead," Griff said. "Jumped down a ravine with his hands cuffed behind his back."

"Whoa." Cam shook his head. "That's crazy."

Griff silently agreed. Going through the woods to reach the cabin took longer than Griff liked, but there was nothing he could do. This was how things went out here in the middle of nowhere. Enforcing the law in the wilderness wasn't easy.

Thankfully, the ambulance was waiting, and the paramedics jumped into action to get Paul transferred from the four-wheeler to the gurney. Soon it was driving away from the cabin, red lights flashing as it headed toward town.

"Where's Maureen?" Griff glanced at Cam as he and Alexis washed Paul's blood from their hands at the cabin sink. Denali followed them inside and stretched out on the floor, watching with her dark eyes. Alexis noticed and filled a dish with water.

"We called her parents," Cameron said. "They were ecstatic to hear from us. And once the girl was cleared by the paramedics, one of our deputies drove her back to Greybull." He turned to Alexis. "She wanted me to let you know how grateful she is that you helped save her life."

"I'm just glad we found her in time." Alexis looked sad. "Too bad we weren't able to save the others."

"I know." Griff reached over to gently pull her close. "I'm sorry you were hurt. Let's get you to the hospital too."

"I'm fine." She leaned against him. "Nothing some sleep won't cure."

He didn't dare tighten his hold, lest he hurt her worse. "Please, Alexis. It's better we know what we're dealing with."

She sighed. "Okay. But I'm telling you, there's no treatment for cracked ribs. And my head doesn't hurt as badly as it did before." She glanced at Denali. "I'm not saying overnight unless Denali can stay too."

He doubted they'd allow that, but he didn't argue. Smoothing his hand down her back, he bit back the need to confess his love. There would be time for that later. "Let's get out of here."

"Gladly," she murmured. "Come, Denali."

"I'll stay until the crime scene techs arrive," Cameron offered.

"Thanks." Griff patted the deputy's shoulder. "I appreciate everything you've done."

"Like letting him get away?" Cam asked bitterly. "What if Paul dies because of this?"

"Paul will be okay. And I don't blame you for his escape. We should have remembered he had the ATV and disabled it." Griff shook his head. "I take full responsibility. I was too worried about Alexis to think clearly."

"I'm glad you came in when you did," Alexis said. "If you hadn't, he'd have shot me."

"See, everything happened for a reason." Griff held Cam's gaze. "We saved Alexis and Maureen. That's what matters."

Cam slowly nodded. "Okay, thanks."

Griff drove Alexis to the hospital, with Denali in the back crate. Once there, he was miffed to realize Alexis had been right. The doc diagnosed her with three cracked ribs and a mild concussion. He discharged her from care, instructing them to return if her symptoms worsened.

"Told you," Alexis said when they were back in the SUV.

"Yeah, yeah." He glanced at her. "Do you want me to drive you to the ranch?"

She sighed and rested her head against the window. "No, let's go to the hotel for now. I need to give Denali a bath. And I'd rather get some sleep before I face the family."

He nodded and made the short drive to the hotel. It was strange to head inside as if nothing had happened.

Once they were in the room, Alexis lowered herself onto the sofa. Denali trotted over to stretch out at her feet. The K9 let out a sigh, lowered her head to the floor, and promptly fell asleep.

Alexis looked up at him. "Griff, can we talk?"

"Of course." He sat beside her, a stab of dread piercing his gut. "You can tell me anything, Alexis. Ah—did Jenkins hurt you?"

"No, nothing like that." She looked down at her hands, then back up at him. "I want you to know I've fallen in love with you."

He stared, wondering if he'd imagined hearing the words he'd wanted to say to her. "Alexis, you've been through a lot. You're injured and need some sleep."

"True, but that doesn't change the fact that I love you." She reached for his hand. "It's okay if you don't feel the same way. Up on that mountain, when I thought you'd been shot, I promised myself that I would tell you how I felt."

His heart filled with hope and longing. "Are you sure? I'm several years older than you. What if you meet someone—"

"Don't," she interrupted. "Don't belittle my feelings because I'm six years younger than you are. If you want to know the truth, I resisted falling for you. I've been burned by long-distance relationships in the past. I wasn't interested in trying again. But you know what? Love doesn't care if you live in Cheyenne and I don't. Love is the most important gift of all. And I love you, Griff."

He felt ashamed. "Alexis, I love you too. So much so that it scares me."

She searched his gaze. "Really? Why does that scare you?"

"I lost my wife two years ago." He tightened his grip on her hand. "It was difficult to go through that. I'd tried to close myself off from my feelings, then you arrived on the scene." He couldn't help but smile. "I knew the first time we met that you had the power to change my life."

"Really?" Her blue eyes held doubt. "You're not just saying that?"

"I love you. I was terrified Jenkins would hurt you before we could get there." He reached up to cup her face in his hand. "I love you so much. And now that we're sitting here, I realize my fears are groundless. You know why?"

She shook her head.

"Because I know now we'll be together in this lifetime for as long as God grants us time on earth, and we'll see each other again in the afterlife."

A smile bloomed on her face. "I couldn't agree

more." She leaned forward and kissed him. He gently pulled her close, taking care not to hurt her.

When their kiss ended, he cradled her close. His gaze landed on the cold pizza. "Are you hungry?"

"Starved," she murmured.

"I'll warm the pizza in the microwave." He pressed a kiss to her temple. "Unless you want me to head out to buy a new one."

"Warmed up pizza is fine." She snuggled close. "But in a minute. Right now, I just want to sit here with you."

"Always." Denali shifted positions on the floor so that she was stretched out over his feet too. He smiled, thinking about the Sullivan K9 ranch and what Alexis had said about avoiding him because she hadn't wanted a long-distance relationship.

He didn't want that either.

"I'll ask my boss if I can be stationed at the ranch," he said.

Alexis tipped her head back to look up at him. "What if he refuses?"

"I'll quit my job and look for something in law enforcement." He reached up to tuck a strand of her hair behind her ear. "I love you, Alexis. I'll do whatever it takes to make you happy."

"Oh, Griff." She smiled. "I love you too. And I'm willing to move to Cheyenne if necessary. Don't quit your job because of me."

"You're more important than a job." He kissed her again. "And I have a feeling my boss won't mind. To be honest, living in a more central location would benefit the bureau. The cost of driving around the state is staggering. Besides, Doug Bridges makes it work."

"Good leverage to use to your advantage," Alexis said with a sly smile. "I like it."

"Me too." He drew her close. "Rest for a bit. Then I'll heat up the pizza."

She nodded and curled against him. As he held her, Griff lifted his gaze to the ceiling, and whispered, "Thank You, Lord Jesus."

"Amen," she echoed.

As peace washed over him, Griff realized God had never left him. His Lord and Savior had been there for him the entire time.

Best of all, he firmly believed Grace was smiling down at them from heaven.

EPILOGUE

Three weeks later . . .

Alexis chafed at being sidelined due to her cracked ribs. They were slowly healing. Walking was fine. Sneezing and coughing hurt like crazy. She leaned on the corral fence, smiling as Denali chased squirrels.

A rumbling sound made her look up to see Logan's plane coming in for a landing. She worried they were taking advantage of Jessica's husband, but Logan loved flying and jumped at the chance to take his bird up in the sky.

"Come, Denali." Pushing off from the fence, she crossed the field toward the runway. She wasn't surprised to see Griff jump down from the plane.

Griff grinned widely and ran toward her. He gently hugged her, always remembering her sore ribs. "I missed you," he murmured against her hair.

"Back at you." She kissed him. Then when Logan loudly cleared his throat, she leaned back to stare at him. "Go away."

"Is that the thanks I get for bringing Griff for the weekend?" Logan pretended to be hurt. "And here I thought I was helping."

"You are, thanks, Logan." Griff gave her another quick kiss before releasing her. "Let's go. I hear Anna has made barbecued ribs for dinner."

"And here I thought you came here to see me," she teased.

"I did." He caught her hand. "And to celebrate closing the Jenkins case." His expression turned serious. "The lab ran all the DNA recovered from the cabin. They matched those of the first three victims, along with yours and Maureen's."

She nodded. Griff had gone back the next day after her abduction to retrieve Tyler's body. The ME had confirmed he died of a broken neck. And when Griff followed up on the other victims, he was able to verify that each of the first three victims had been eating or buying baked goods when they were taken. He'd learned that Tyler had worked as a freelance delivery driver, which was why he'd been in different cities around the state. He hadn't delivered to the ranch, but he very well could have. Finally, Griff mentioned they'd found a tiny closet in the bakery that was once owned and operated by Tyler Jenkins's mother.

Alexis hadn't seen it, but Griff had described the scratch marks in the wall. And the blood stains soaked into the wooden floor had matched Tyler's. As a child, he must have smelled the baked goods his mother made the entire time he was locked in the closet.

In a way, she understood why Tyler had gone insane. It was just too bad three young women had to pay the price of his madness.

"One more thing I uncovered," Griff said as they headed to the main ranch house. "Turns out, Tyler's mother was killed by the oldest son in a murder suicide. In talking to Cheri, we think that was the inciting incident that sent Tyler over the edge, as it happened just three months before Josie Allen went missing."

"Wow." She shook her head. "Tyler lived a tortured life, and that's sad. But I'm glad he can't hurt anyone else."

"Me too."

She knew something was up when a pack of dogs came running from the other side of the house. She recognized them as her siblings K9s, including Bear the chocolate lab who was the newest member of the group, having been rescued by Owen

Ross and his new wife, Emily. The couple had gotten married in late June and stayed at the ranch part time to train Bear to become a search and rescue K9.

Denali quickly ran to join them. The dogs jumped and played with abandon, one of the few times they were given free rein.

Griff held the door open for her. Somehow, Logan had gotten into the main ranch house before them and stood with the rest of her family, looking suspiciously happy.

She hung back, glancing at Griff. "You didn't invite them all on purpose, did you?"

His green eyes widened with innocence. "Who me?" Before she could say anything more, he dropped to one knee and held out a ring. "Alexis, will you please marry me?"

Her family went silent for a long moment, waiting for her response. As annoyed as she was to have an audience, she had no intention of disappointing them.

"Yes, Griff. I'd be honored to marry you." Her siblings burst into a round of applause, Owen whistling loudly between his fingers.

"I love you." Griff stood and slipped the ring on her finger. He drew her close and kissed her.

"There must be something in the water around

here," Joel complained. "Everyone's getting hitched."

"Not me, bro." Justin shook his head. "We'd better fill our canteens elsewhere."

"I'm on board with that plan," Trevor agreed. Kendra elbowed him in the ribs.

"Knock it off," Chase said. He pulled his pregnant wife close. "You don't know what you're missing."

"Another wedding." Kendra sighed. "It's so romantic."

Alexis broke off from the kiss and turned to the youngest Sullivan. "Kendra, will you please be my maid of honor?"

"Really?" Kenda's eyes brightened. "That would be great."

"One more thing." Chase raised his voice to be heard over the din. "I got the DNA results from the bone fragment Alexis and Denali found on the mountain. It's a match for the pilot who crashed the plane, killing our parents."

The pilot. Despite finding it not too far from where Tyler's victims had been buried, Alexis hadn't really expected the bone fragment to be significant.

But it was.

"Are you okay?" Griff asked in a low voice as the rest of the family began to debate what may have happened that fateful day.

"Yes, but it's a shock." She leaned against Griff. "We'll have to take Denali back up to that area soon. There could be more remains up there."

"Okay with me." Griff pressed a kiss to her temple. "But don't make me wait too long to marry you. I finally got my boss to agree that I can work remotely. That means I can live here with you once we tie the knot."

She brightened. "That's wonderful news!"

"Yeah." He grinned down at her. "I love you, Alexis."

"I love you too." She kissed him again and pushed the mystery surrounding their parents' plane crash from her mind.

Life was short and not to be taken for granted. Tyler had come close to killing her, she wasn't going to wait to marry Griff. She would cherish each day they had together.

The love they shared was a gift from God.

I HOPE you enjoyed Alexis and Griff's story in *Scent of Death*. Are you ready to read about Joel and Trina in *Scent of Fury*? Click here!

DEAR READER

Thanks for reading *Scent of Death*! I hope you enjoyed Alexis and Griff's story. I'm having so much fun writing about the Sullivan family. I hope you are enjoying them as much as I am. And please stay tuned for *Scent of Fury*, which will be Joel and Trina's story. You won't want to miss that one.

Don't forget, you can purchase ebooks or audiobooks directly from my website and will receive a 15% discount by using the code **LauraScott15.**

I adore hearing from my readers! I can be found through my website at https://www.laurascottbooks.com, via Facebook at https://www.facebook.com/LauraScottBooks, Instagram at https://www.instagram.com/laurascottbooks/, and Twitter https://twitter.com/laurascottbooks. Please take a moment to subscribe to my YouTube channel at youtube.-

com/@LauraScottBooks-wr1xl?sub_confirmation=1. Also take a moment to sign up for my monthly newsletter to learn about my new book releases! All subscribers receive a free novella not available for purchase on any platform.

Until next time,

Laura Scott

PS. Keep reading for a sneak peek of *Scent of Fury* ...

SCENT OF FURY

Chapter One

A heavy thudding sound woke Trina Warren from sleep. Blinking in the dim light, she frowned, straining to listen. It took a moment to remember she shared her house with her eight-year-old nephew, Ben. The boy was her responsibility now that her older sister had passed away from a tragic biking accident back in May. With a grimace, Trina jumped out of bed, shoved her feet into a pair of slippers, and opened the door to the hallway.

Ben's previously closed bedroom door hung ajar.

"Ben? Is everything okay?" She pushed his door open, expecting to see him in bed, but the room was empty.

A shiver of panic snaked down her spine. "Ben? Where are you?"

No response. Moving quickly through her small three-bedroom house, it didn't take long for her to verify the boy was nowhere to be found.

Her stomach knotted as she hurried back to Ben's room. Flipping on the light switch, she scanned the room. As usual, it was a mess, but she grimly realized his shoes and favorite long-sleeved western-style shirt were missing. Along with the brand-new school backpack she'd purchased for him last week.

A sense of dread seeped into her bones. Ben had been struggling with the loss of his mother and with moving from Laramie to Cody. Her sister had lived in an apartment after her divorce from Ben's father who had taken off when Ben was five. At the time, Trina had thought bringing Ben to live at her house, giving him a fresh start here in Cody, had been the better option.

Now she wasn't so sure.

Praying he hadn't done anything stupid, she spun around and bolted outside. At five thirty in the morning, dawn was just breaking over the horizon. Raking her gaze over the area, she searched for him. "Ben! Ben, where are you?"

The early morning breeze rustled the leaves on the trees. Dew on the grass dampened her slippers.

Her home was in the northwest corner of Cody, close to the local nature trail. Ben had looked at her in disgust when she'd suggested hiking the trail a few days ago. Maybe because of the way his mother had died in a mountain bike accident? She wasn't sure what he'd been thinking. Ben hadn't opened up to her. She wasn't even sure he opened up to his psychologist.

Would he have gone for an early morning hike on his own?

It didn't seem likely, but she wasn't sure where else he'd gone. Swallowing hard, she turned and ran back inside. She swapped her slippers for hiking boots and drew on a sweatshirt. Early mornings in August could be chilly. First, she'd go through the neighborhood, then check the trail. Maybe he hadn't gone far.

Trina grabbed her phone, then paused when she noticed one of the kitchen cabinet doors was open. Obviously, Ben had taken more than just his backpack. She turned and headed back outside. Considering he'd taken his backpack, she didn't really think he'd be in the neighborhood, but she forced herself to walk up and down the streets anyway. When she didn't find him, she headed through her backyard to the shortcut that would take her to the nature trail.

If she didn't find Ben soon, she would call the

Sullivans for help. She'd gone to high school with the twins, Joel and Justin Sullivan. At one time, she'd harbored a crush on Joel, but the day she'd hoped to ask him to homecoming, she'd found him with Bethany, one of the high school cheerleaders. They'd made a striking pair with Joel's dark hair and Bethany's long blond tresses. Trina with her red hair and freckles looked like Peppermint Patty from the Snoopy cartoon, so she'd kept her distance after that.

Still, the family was well known throughout the region for their search and rescue services. Trina walked along the path, concerned because there were points where the trail paralleled the path of the Shoshone River, which flowed rapidly enough to be dangerous.

Especially for a child who hadn't grown up in the area.

"Ben!" She followed the trail to the south, hoping that was the direction he'd taken. But really, he could have gone either way.

After ten minutes with not seeing him, she turned and ran in the opposite direction. How far could an eight-year-old walk anyway? She had no idea.

The incline was steeper along the north path, and after a few minutes, she gave up. Her voice was hoarse from yelling his name. If Ben hadn't stayed on the trail, he could have been anywhere.

She pulled out her phone and called the Sullivan ranch. Even at barely six in the morning, her call was quickly answered by a female voice. "Sullivan K9 Search and Rescue."

"Good morning. My name is Trina Warren, and my eight-year-old nephew, Ben Warren, is missing. I—we live in Cody. I went to school with Joel and Justin and need help, fast."

"Of course. Joel and Royal are free to help." The woman's tone was cheerful yet calm. "What's your address?"

Trina rattled off the information.

"Great. I'll give him your contact information, okay? He'll call when he's on the road."

"Thank you." Knowing help was on the way brought a wave of relief. After pocketing her phone, she decided to keep going up the path. After all, she knew it would take almost forty-five minutes for Joel to get there.

Maybe she'd find Ben before then.

She continued walking, scanning both sides of the path for any sign of Ben. Her earlier annoyance with his going off on his own had morphed into fear. What if he'd tripped, fallen, and hit his head? Her sister, Evie, had died of a severe head injury.

She couldn't bear the thought of losing Ben the same way.

For a moment, she thought of Ben's father. Brian Ashland had made it clear he had no desire to be married or tied down to a child. Evie had gotten pregnant right after high school. Brian had gotten a job in Laramie, so Evie and Ben had moved there too. They'd gotten married, but things had not gone well for the young couple. Trina hadn't been surprised when Brian left. Evie had been glad to be rid of him, having confided that Brian's drinking had gotten worse over the years, and when he was drunk, he slapped her around. In Evie's eyes, she was better off without him.

The one who'd suffered the most was Ben. As a five-year-old, he hadn't understood the undercurrents between his parents. One day his father was there, the next Brian was gone.

Her phone rang, startling her. Pulling it from her pocket, she quickly answered. "Hello?"

"Trina? Is that you?"

Joel's husky voice almost brought tears to her eyes. Until that moment, she'd carried the weight of Ben's absence alone. "Yes, it's me. Sorry, my voice is hoarse. I've been hiking the trail calling for Ben."

"Understandable," Joel said reassuringly. "I'm on my way, should be there in fifteen minutes or so."

"Thank you." He'd made good time, and she turned to head back home. There was no point in wasting more time. She knew Joel's K9, Royal, would be able to find Ben.

"I'll need dirty socks or T-shirts from your nephew to use as a scent source for Royal," Joel said.

"Trust me, his room has plenty of dirty clothes strewn about." She tried to smile, but fresh tears pricked her eyes instead. "I'm heading home now."

"Sounds good. Don't worry, my black lab Royal is a great tracker."

"I'm glad." She swiped at her face. "See you soon."

"Soon," he echoed, before ending the call. Shoving her phone back into her pocket, she picked up the pace. She was convinced Joel and his K9 would find Ben. Especially if the boy had left the trail.

Ben would be okay. Tired, hungry, and maybe sore if he'd fallen, but he'd be fine.

She couldn't bear the thought of finding the young boy seriously hurt or worse.

Joel used his thumb to end the call with Trina. He remembered her from high school, although they hadn't shared many classes. She'd been a quiet, shy girl who'd preferred books over people.

He hadn't known her nephew was staying with her and wondered if that was a temporary summer vacation kind of thing or something more permanent. Not that it mattered. A missing child was always a high priority.

His phone rang again, but this time, it was Lisa's name on the screen. With a low groan, he quickly hit the end-call button, sending her to voice mail. This was the third time she'd called this week. It had been a mistake to give Lisa Schilling his number. The strikingly beautiful female hiker he and Royal had found and rescued over a month ago now had mistaken his concern for her welfare as something more. She'd repeatedly asked him to lunch and dinner. He'd tried to let her down gently, but she had continued calling anyway. He'd been even more concerned when she'd let him know she'd moved to Wyoming from Arizona. Again, he'd told her he was busy with SAR work, but she claimed she loved it here.

He'd suspected she'd moved for him.

Justin told him to block her number. And after this week, he was on board with that plan. Why was she calling him so early in the morning anyway? Was there a problem of some sort? He resisted the urge to call her back. More likely she was being persistent, accustomed to getting her way. Bethany, the girl he'd dated in high school, had been the same way. As if beauty alone was all that mattered.

Whatever. He'd deal with her later. For now, he had work to do.

Keeping his foot planted on the accelerator, he pushed the speed limit, hoping there weren't any state patrol cars in the area. The sense of urgency to get to Cody was difficult to ignore.

As if sensing his tension, Royal pressed his nose against the wire mesh of the crate. Joel glanced at the dog in the rearview mirror. "Soon, boy. We'll be there soon."

Royal's tail thumped against the bottom of the crate in response.

Trina's home was a small ranch with light-green siding that looked as if it may have been there for decades. The yard was neatly tended. Flowery bushes framed the front door, a water hose lying on the ground nearby. He pulled into the driveway and killed the engine. The front door opened as he slid out from behind the wheel, hitting the button to release the back hatch.

"Hi, Joel, it's good to see you again." Trina's expression was strained as she approached. She held a plastic bag in one hand. She stepped forward to envelop him in a friendly embrace. "Thank you for getting here so quickly."

"Of course." He hugged her back, then stepped to the side so Royal could jump down. He turned to face her. "Trina, will you please come closer?"

"Sure." She eyed him warily as she did so.

He knelt beside Royal and took Trina's hand. "Friend, Royal. Trina is a friend."

Royal sniffed her hand, then his tail wagged from side to side. Trina's expression softened as she stroked the lab's soft, glossy black fur with her free hand. "You're a good boy, huh?"

"Yep." He smiled and rose to his feet. "As I said, Royal is very good at finding lost people. Is that Ben's clothing?"

"Yes." She handed the bag to him. "Dirty socks and T-shirts."

"Perfect. Give me a minute to get Royal ready." He pulled a fluorescent vest from the compartment beneath the crate and slipped it over Royal's torso. Then he filled a bowl with water and offered it to his K9.

Royal lapped the water, then lifted his head to stare up at him with large expectant brown eyes.

"Are you ready? Huh, boy?" He injected enthusiasm into his tone to excite his dog. Searches were viewed as a game. The higher the play-and-prey drive in a K9, the better they performed. Shoving the collapsible bowl into the backpack, he shouldered the pack and opened the scent bag. "This is Ben. Ben! Search Ben!"

Royal buried his snout in the clothing, his tail wagging from side to side with anticipation. Then the lab whirled and began sniffing along the sidewalk.

"Ben's been living here with me since June," Trina said. "My sister passed away." Her brown eyes filled with grief. "I'm going through the process of formally adopting Ben, but he's not exactly thrilled to be here with me."

He nodded, his heart going out to her. It couldn't be easy to have a young boy dropped into your lap. "If he's not familiar with the area, he probably took a walk and got himself lost along the way."

"Maybe." She chewed her lower lip. "But I think he may have run away. He took his new backpack with him. When I was gathering his dirty clothes, I noticed some other things were missing, like his favorite handheld video game. The cabinet door was open, too, so he may have grabbed a snack."

"I see." He gestured toward Royal who sat at the front door and barked. "That's Royal's first alert. I need to reward him before we keep going."

Trina glanced at her watch, gnawing on her lip again. "Okay. But Ben's been gone now for ninety minutes."

"We'll find him." Joel empathized with her concern. He and his twin had run wild when they were eight, but that was because their parents had too many kids to watch them like hawks. And growing up on the dude ranch had given them free rein to do what they wanted. Yet he knew that wasn't how parents handled their kids these days. He was sure Ben had rarely been out of Trina's sight.

He hurried over to reward Royal with his stuffed beaver. The dog leaped into the air to catch the beaver and ran around with the toy in his mouth. After a moment, he called the dog back and held out his palm. "Hand."

Royal regurgitated the stuffed beaver into his palm. Then he stared up at Joel, waiting for the next command.

"Search! Search Ben!"

Anxious to please, Royal turned and began sniffing around the yard. When the dog trotted around back, he quickly followed. Trina caught up, her gaze hopeful as she watched Royal work.

It didn't take long for Royal to head for the gap between the trees along the back of the yard. He glanced questioningly at Trina, who nodded.

"Yes, this is the shortcut to the hiking trail." She swallowed hard. "I checked both directions, calling out to Ben, but he didn't respond."

"Royal is on the scent." He wanted to reassure

her they'd find Ben alive and unhurt, but he couldn't. He'd done too many of these search and rescue missions to know that the outcome wasn't always positive.

Not that he had any intention of telling her that. Best to stay positive. Even if the eight-year-old had decided to run away, by now he was probably tired, hungry, and more than ready to return home.

Royal turned north on the trail, his tail waving back and forth as the lab followed the scent. The trail went up a steep incline but eventually leveled off. He glanced at Trina. "Have you and Ben come this way before?"

"Never." She wrinkled her nose. "I suggested hiking, but Ben looked at me as if I had two heads. His mother died from a mountain biking accident, which might be part of the reason he turned me down. He's still grieving over his loss."

"Of course, he is," Joel agreed. "It wasn't easy losing our parents when we were adults. It must be ten times harder for a child."

"I have him in counseling, but he tries to weasel out of attending his sessions." She sighed. "He makes me feel bad for insisting he go. I know it's for his own good, but he gets so angry with me."

"Yeah, well, anger is part of the grief process too." He looped his arm around her shoulders. "He'll come around."

"Will he?" She frowned and leaned against him for a moment, then she ran her fingers through her straight bright-red hair. "Sorry, it's just hard to know if I'm doing the right thing for him."

"You are." He squeezed her again, then released her. He watched as Royal continued on the path, then abruptly turned to the right. His K9 sniffed near a park bench, sat, and let out a sharp bark. "That's his alert!"

Trina broke away and ran toward Royal. "Ben? Where are you?"

Joel examined the park bench area, noticing there were blue and white sprinkle crumbs embedded in the dirt. "Do you think Ben took cookies of some kind?"

Trina frowned, spotting the sprinkles. Then her expression cleared. "Blueberry Pop-Tarts. He wanted them from the store, and while they're not exactly healthy, I gave in. The cupboard door was open this morning. I hadn't taken the time to see what he'd grabbed." She rubbed her eyes. "I'm glad he ate something."

"I agree, finding sprinkles is reassuring. Good boy, Royal! Good boy!" He tossed the stuffed beaver again. Royal sprinted after it.

"Your dog really can track his scent," she murmured. "I honestly wasn't convinced."

"A lot of people say that." He was used to the skeptics. "But our K9s are the real deal."

A faint smile tugged at the corner of her mouth. "Thanks. I owe you big time."

He waved that off. "The fee is a bag of dog food, if you can afford it. If not, don't worry, we tend to let the dog food fee slide when kids are involved."

"I can afford it." She raked her fingers through her hair again. "I write books, which surprisingly do pretty well."

"Really?" He hadn't known that. He opened his mouth to ask more, but she held up her hand to stop him.

"Before you ask, no, I'm sure you haven't read any of them. I write cozy mystery books set in a small Montana town. My readers are mostly women, although I do have some male fans. But I'm sure they're not your type of story." She sighed, and added, "I was so glad I had a job that enabled me to work from home so I could be around for Ben, but that obviously hasn't worked. Ben still took off without telling me."

"It's not your fault." He could tell she believed it was. She was right that he wasn't a big reader, but he filed the information away for later. He didn't mind a good mystery. But now it was time to get back to work. "Here, Royal." He called his dog over and held out his hand for the beaver. "Search. Search Ben!"

Royal lowered his nose to the ground, but this time, rather than following the path, he trotted into the woods. Joel glanced at Trina, then followed his K9.

"This is why he got lost," Trina muttered. "Why didn't he stay on the path?"

"Maybe he saw an elk or deer." They weren't that far from the Absaroka Mountains, home to all sorts of wildlife. "Kids that age are curious."

"Maybe." Trina didn't look convinced.

Royal continued moving along a curvy path through the woods. He could easily imagine an eight-year-old taking this route, around trees and over fallen logs. His K9 didn't hesitate or backtrack, so he knew Royal was still on the scent.

The longer they walked, the deeper the worry lines became etched in Trina's face. She gestured to a break in the trees. "The river isn't far from here. What if he fell in the water? I don't even know if Ben can swim! He has swim trunks, but that doesn't mean he can survive falling in the river!"

"Easy," he cautioned. "Royal will help us find him. Trust the process, okay?"

"I can't lose him," Trina whispered in a low, agonizing tone. "I just can't."

"Have faith in God," he encouraged. When she frowned, he realized she wasn't a believer. "I have faith, Trina. I believe God will watch over him."

"The way He watched over my sister, Evie?" Her tone reeked of bitterness. "Yeah, no thanks."

He decided to let it go. This wasn't the time to have this conversation. He kept his gaze focused on Royal's progress. He understood how difficult it was to get past anger and grief after losing a loved one. He and his eight siblings had struggled after losing their parents five and a half years ago. It was only after his parents had died in a plane crash that the siblings had gotten together and turned the former luxury dude ranch into a search and rescue operation.

They all lived on the ranch now, taking over the ten guest cabins. They had their own space, but their siblings were also close at hand if needed. And their faith had grown stronger over the years.

Royal made another abrupt turn, this time heading away from the river. Joel reached over to grab Trina's hand when she stumbled while trying to keep up. "Are you okay?"

"Fine. I didn't expect that." She waved at the dog. "I was convinced he was heading to the river."

"This is why we stay back and let our K9 take the lead." He held her hand for a long moment before releasing it. "We don't do anything to influence the dog one way or the other. Royal is following Ben's scent."

"I believe you, Joel, but where is he?" Trina sounded frustrated. "I don't see Ben anywhere."

He wasn't sure what to say because she was right. The hour was still early enough that there were no kids in the area. He saw a female jogger and an older man wearing a cowboy hat and using a walking stick, but even with the tourist season in full swing, the trail wasn't busy.

Then he saw a car driving past. There was too much foliage to see much, but he had to assume there was a road up ahead.

His spirits sank when Royal headed straight through the brush. When they came out on the other side, he saw the road. It appeared to lead to another subdivision.

Royal trotted faster now, sniffing along the side of the road.

"Auntie Trina!" The young voice came from around the corner of the street.

"Ben?" Trina increased her pace. "Ben! I'm here!"

A young kid appeared around the corner, running toward them. Royal lifted his head and sniffed the air. Joel was about to call off the dog when a sharp crack of gunfire echoed through the area.

"Ben!" Trina pulled Ben close, curling her body over the boy, half carrying him to the shelter of the trees. Royal let out a sharp bark, either in warning to the gunman or to alert on his find.

Joel leaned over to grab Royal's vest, pulling the dog to the woods too. He crouched in front of Royal, Trina, and Ben and scanned the area. Long seconds turned into a full minute. Had that been a random gunshot?

Or were Trina and Ben in danger?

www.ingramcontent.com/pod-product-compliance
Lightning Source LLC
Chambersburg PA
CBHW070626300726
48975CB00006B/1936